Lies to Live By

Lies to Live By

Lois Beardslee

Michigan State University Press
East Lansing

∞ The paper used in this publication meets the minimum requirements
of ANSI/NISO Z39.48-1992 (R 1997) (Permanence of Paper).
Michigan State University Press
East Lansing, Michigan 48823-5245

Printed and bound in the United States of America.
09 08 07 06 05 04 03 1 2 3 4 5 6 7 8 9 10

LIBRARY OF CONGRESS CATALOGING-IN-PUBLICATION DATA

Beardslee, Lois.
    Lies to live by / Lois Beardslee.
        p. cm.
    ISBN 0-87013-663-1 (pbk. : alk. paper)
    1. Ojibwa Indians—Social life and customs. 2. Ojibwa Indians—Folklore.
I. Title.
    E99.C6 .B42 2003
398.2′089′973—dc21

                                                            2002153575

Book and cover design by Sans Serif Inc.
Cover art is a detail from *Potty Training, Dixon Island* by Lois Beardslee,
Acrylic, 23 × 31.

Visit Michigan State University Press on the World Wide Web at:
www.msupress.msu.edu

CONTENTS

Pragmatism as a Source of Understanding

Long after the gingerbread house provided an evening's entertainment for three giggling teenage girls, the cottage sat petrifying on the kitchen counter. Colorful and fanciful, it remained irresistible. Gumdrop shingles slowly disappeared and icing shrubbery bore distinct teeth marks. ("Someone topped it for a Christmas tree, Mom.") Emulating his older models, a two-year-old worked the browse line on an already chewed cedar tree and moved on to a sugary doorknob.

"Leave it there," I insisted. "There are witches living in those things. They get upset when you eat their houses." The pragmatic reality of the Hansel and Gretel story suddenly transposed itself from Europe hundreds of years ago to my northern Michigan modern kitchen. The creative challenge of keeping one's children from eating the goodies has remained culturally intact.

For years the challenge I have carved out for myself is to convey that same sense of immediacy on behalf of northern Woodland Indian traditions. More pragmatic than mystic, our characters and the stories about them remained culturally intact because they are still applicable. They teach our children a system of behavioral guidelines and cultural values. They teach them how to stay out of trouble or avoid being hurt. They explain things as rudimentary as, "No, the first time," or avoiding gluttony. The stories also preserve nuts-and-bolts information about how to do things the right way, such as peeling a tree and building a temporary bark shelter.

Reading between the lines and finding pragmatic messages is the best way to open up understanding of Native traditions to audiences. Some basic human needs (such as keeping the kids from eating the goodies) transcend cultural boundaries, binding us all together. Yet there is beauty in the variety with which we have chosen to embellish our solutions to those issues. Among the Woodland Natives, these stories varied from village to village, reflecting the humor, creativity, and specific needs of each storyteller.

We have dozens of solutions to the problem of keeping our children from eating the gingerbread house. They manifest themselves in a variety of characters and situations, have evolved fluidly throughout the years, and continue to do so. Obviously, all aspects of Native cultures are not open books. However, I like to think that Native American artists and cultural interpreters are faced with a more receptive audience today than in our historic past. No one can share our traditions more sensitively and lucidly than we can. We represent less than one-half of one percent of this nation's population. It is important that our rich and varied contributions to American culture are shared with the public in a respectful and understanding way.

Lies to Live By

To Mike Petoskey

I am often asked if the Woodland Indians of the Great Lakes have a storyteller character, similar to the Storyteller dolls of the Southwest. Sometimes, in the interest of brevity, I mention Dibawjimot. Any Chippewa (Ojibwe) or Ottawa (Odawa) Indian, hard-pressed would interpret this character as "the storyteller."

In reality, Dibawjimot is Grandmother's companion. Grandmother, or Nokomis, is a character who raised the youngest of four half-spirit/half-human brothers who occur in our oral history and stories. She represents the all-caring presence and continuity of family and other authority figures. She is part of the traditional extended family. It is in the setting of her wigwam and camp that many of our "how come" stories take place.

Dibawjimot, the Storyteller

Even though she is old, Nokomis is still busy and attractive. Dibawjimot, her suitor, is a typical older widower. He talks maybe a little bit too much, about the old ways, about how to do things the right way. He sometimes gives his advice and opinions when they are not necessarily sought by his young charges, much to their chagrin. Often he speaks in anecdotes and euphemisms.

We are taught that, like the youths of our oral history, we will understand the wisdom that Dibawjimot shares only as we grow older and have more life experiences. Even adults experience moments of revelation, times when we reflect upon what we have been told by Dibawjimot or another elder.

Sometimes I am asked if I learned my traditional stories from another storyteller. Again, in the interest of brevity, I make reference to a great uncle, Leonard Mopishwash, who was a great talker. Uncle was not known within the community as a storyteller. He was merely a talker. He enjoyed sharing his time with youngsters (including my parents) and showing us how to do things. He often punctuated his stories with small figures and masks made out of sticks, birch bark, and even paper plates. His hands were always moving. He talked nonstop while we cleaned fish, plucked the feathers out of ducks for dinner, or butchered a deer.

I cannot think of Dibawjimot without visualizing my uncle. I suspect that he was as alert, active, and wiry. Like Dibawjimot's advice, Uncle's stories often came down to me in ninety seconds or less. I have learned details from other people as well. It has taken a lifetime of experiences and cultural learning to put the bits and pieces together into the stories that I tell today. That is, I suppose, the definition of belonging to one cultural group or another. I never stop learning.

Minan is the Ojibwe word for berries. Some berries are named for what they look like. Strawberries are really called "heart berries," or *oday-minan*. Raspberries are *miskiwiiminan*—"blood berries." As children, after we had carried them around in our hands for too long, we used to call them *miskiwiiwiminan, or* "bloody berries."

The word for blueberries is simply *minan*— "berries." Blueberries are the most important wild fruit in the subarctic. People who have never been north of the southern Great Lakes during late summer and autumn cannot fathom how extensively *minan* grow. They are not picked a handful at a time. They grow in such large, thick, bushy swaths that women and children can gather huge quantities of them in only a few hours. *Minan* have such a high content of sugar and pectin that they stay intact and harvestable from mid-August until hard frost. Even if the berries dry on the bushes, they are still harvestable and edible. In the old days, it was not uncommon for northern Ojibwe to trade blueberries for corn, beans, and squash with their cousins to the south.

Minan

My family has a camp in the far north. In September we bake as many as a half-dozen blueberry pies in one day. Big, full, bulging pies. We scoop up the *minan* with our fingers stretched out, raking them up by the handful, eating at least as many as we bring home. I have always told my children that I have only one berry-picking rule: for every berry you put in the bucket, you must put two in your mouth. A favorite game is to eat them like bears, on all fours, no hands.

We are not alone when we pick our berries. Sometimes the dog's ears perk up. We look up, to stare off into the bush where a lumbering, crashing sound in the woods has come to a sudden stop. Sometimes we pick so quietly that the bears happen upon us. They watch us, then silently, cautiously back away. It is their favorite blueberry spot, too. On the way home, we see their loose, blue-stained stools on the dusty openness of the bush trail. It seems that we both enjoy and depend upon *minan* so much that we risk this uncomfortable interaction with one another.

We have a story about Minan, the Blueberry Boy. He wandered off from his sister and his mother. Like most small children, he didn't understand the importance of the task of gathering berries for the long winter ahead. He ate so many berries that he turned into a bear, and his family did not recognize him.

I gaze over at my own little blue-toothed Minan and urge him to stay a little closer to me and the dog. The big St. Bernard cross is lying down, lapping up blueberries with her tongue. When the buckets are full, we join her for a last-minute feast, on all fours, no hands. Mmmmmmm-*minan*.

According to tradition, we Ojibwe women consider ourselves "keepers of the water." It is a title we bestow upon ourselves, an honor. It was once a pragmatic term, we are certain, a reference to the fact that we once hauled it for cooking and cleaning in the family camps. There is honor in the division of labor between the sexes and between people of different ages and abilities. It means that we each have value. Our culture cannot survive without each and every one of us.

As keepers of the water in the home, we made sure that our nearby water supply was not defiled with waste and runoff. We instructed the children carefully in the disposal of wash water and other wastes so that they could do their daily chores with minimal supervision. No one can live without water and yet it becomes spoiled so easily, with the tiniest contamination.

Keepers of the Water

In ceremonial and teaching contexts, it is the women only who handle the water. This is to remind all of us of the important roles that women play in our everyday lives, families, and society, as well as in our history.

Some elders say that our Mother Earth was populated with the *Anishnabeg,* or human beings, by the first woman, Kiishigokwe. She is the bringer of all life, not just human life. Her name means Cloud Woman. She exists in the air, in great sweeping cloud banks, and in mists. On warm days, she takes up the moisture from the lakes surrounding our homes and stores it in the breezes. She releases it to the plants and the lake basins in the form of life-giving precipitation. The water is continually recycled and reused, always changing forms, not unlike Kiishigokwe. She takes on many personifications and has the power of multiplicity—she can be in many places at one time. We do not distinguish between her earthly personification (present within all Ojibwe women) and her historic, or supernatural identity. Her role is a beneficial and loving one. She is, in her manner of generosity and behavior, a role model for all *Anishnabe* women. Like Kiishigokwe, we make essential contributions to the life cycle. We are the keepers of the water.

In the dimmest early light of day, young Bidawbn sat on the rocks above the water talking to Maang (Loon). Next to her, the canoe was pulled up into a soft indentation of sand along the shore. She was careful never to drag it over sharp rocks. She could not float over the water without the canoe. She needed it to catch fish to help her parents nourish the family. It was a job she normally enjoyed, but she had not been successful for several days.

Maang, she knew, was always successful. He did not hesitate to share his wisdom on the art of fishing. Bidawbn leaned far out over the water, until only a single moccasined toe held firm to a shallow crevice in the granite outcropping. The trickster bird stretched its neck upward to whisper into the young, inexperienced ear.

Sneaking Up on a Fish

With only a few strategic words, Maang talked the girl into riding the lake on his back. They glided silently into the water, and she was gone.

The water surface was calm. She leaned carefully to one side to gaze down past his spotted back, into the shadow cast by his wide body, deep into the water. "Think like a fish," Maang insisted. "Know where they are and when and why. Sneak up on the fish, and they will give themselves to you." He slowly, imperceptibly lowered himself into the water, until his eyes were submerged. Bidawbn's face became submerged also. She did not panic. She found herself enjoying this calm, quiet fishing lesson. Her hair flowed back behind her as they dove, together. The motion was comforting.

She is there still, Bidawbn, the oldest daughter. She is an excellent fisher, but she can no longer bring the fish home to her waiting family. She is a bit frustrated by her lack of human speech. She calls and trills when the family canoes come near. She shows us where the fish are waiting to be caught, dipping and submerging, reemerging and flapping her wings. We find and keep her spotted feathers when they wash up on the downwind beaches.

There is a favorite rock outcropping below the surface of the lake where the walleye sometimes come to eat in the late afternoon. Once, returning from town with children, dog, and groceries in the boat, we decided to troll our fishing lines past that spot. My sixteen-year-old daughter immediately hooked a big fish. After about three cranks, the pin broke on the handle of the fishing reel. We stopped the boat, while she patiently wound in all the line by hand. Eventually, she landed a twenty-four-inch walleye. Because there was no tension on the line, the fish did not put up a fight until the very last few feet. That is one reason that our ancestors were so successful at fishing by hand without graphite poles—they knew how to sneak up on the fish. Thank you, Bidawbn.

There is an ancient word from the Ojibwe language that has fallen into disuse. It has been a good forty years since I heard it used. The word is *maagde*. It means disconcerted. It is a verb form that is difficult for me to describe, because it comes across to the English reader as an adjective.

As a child, I had heard the word used in reference to the *manidog*, or spirits, as in *maagde manido*, a concerned, disturbed, even slightly perturbed spirit—but never an angry spirit. When characters have been described to me in our stories throughout the years, they have all been likeable, even the most disagreeable ones. There is no such thing as a *matchi manido*, which translates as "bad spirit." That concept is a relic of early contact times, when Renaissance-era European concepts of good and  **Big Water** evil were overlaid upon our own traditional perceptions of the spirits. Some confusion about Native relationships with "spirits" surely resulted from differences in culture, not just language. All of our traditional characters have human characteristics. To condemn them would be to condemn ourselves.

There is a group of spirits called the *michigaamigag*—underwater monsters who live in every lake, stream, and underground seep. They are monsters in the real sense of the word, in that they are made up of more than one creature. Many of them are *michikiniibigag*, snakes with antlers, whose exploits are sometimes humorous. Because of their absurd combination of sinuous and rigid body parts, they tend to get their antlers stuck between rocks. The most famous of the *michigaamigag* is Mishii Bizhou, the underwater panther with antlers, who waves his huge cattail to make lethal waves on the Great Lakes. He is *not* an evil spirit. He and his cohorts have a job to do. They keep an eye on the weather and the resources and make sure that greedy fishermen get off of the lake. If fisher-men do not heed the warnings of wind, waves, or thin ice, the *michigaamigag* are obligated to remove them from the gene pool. They are the original ecological fanatics. We speak of them at once tongue in cheek and equally with reverence. They seem less humorous when real names and faces are put to the victims—so often Indian youths on snowmobiles on the thin ice, winter-bound and bored on their waterfront homes—not greedy at all, just inexperienced, lacking in mentorship.

I once heard another Ojibwe storyteller tell an audience: "There were all sorts of things out there that were so horrible that they were indescribable by our parents and grandparents. They served a purpose. They kept us scared. They kept us alive. They kept us out of dangerous places." Indeed, when we speak of these monsters, we do so not as the ignorant, childlike fools described by early ethnographers, but rather as wizened, con-niving parents. They are very real to us, because we live on and with the water. They are absolutely necessary. These characters and their stories are surrogate mentors, when we can't be with our children to protect them.

We have many stories that deal with drowning. Some are gruesome. Others are beautiful. The gruesome stories are pre-ventive in nature. The lovely ones are for the survivors. Some describe an alternate family life under the water. These stories are a natural consequence of lifestyles intertwined with water resources.

In a few hours, I hope to spend an hour and a half rolling my fourteen-foot boat downhill over water-worn logs onto Lake Su-perior's shore. I plan to spend some time at my island camp and put it into sorts for the long winter. It is only a few days until Halloween, and *Gitchiigami* can be deadly. I will travel miles over depths of several hundred feet, thirty miles each way down the coast from the next dwelling.

It has been dead calm for many days, and I hope that the winds will let me launch. If not, I will pull the boat farther north to another family camp on an inland lake. The lake is only a few miles across, and I can launch in the wind. Still, to reach the dwelling, I will pass over depths of 100 feet on a body of water that has for many weeks been colder than Superior's tremendous heat holding mass. Hypothermia can kill in only minutes, and my camp is the only one on the lake, far from the nearest Indian town of one hundred.

We are not fools. We will not risk our lives. My family remains cautious, and we draw upon generations of experience living among these big lakes. The *manidog,* the spirits, are very real to me at this moment—as educators, protectors, and symbols of common sense and caution. Sad consequences are the stuff that legends are made of. I am elated to slip away from my work, the phone, the traffic; but I am, well, disconcerted.

I feel vindicated.

For seventeen years I have shared with my children stories of my childhood, tales of rare, once-or-twice-in-a-lifetime events and situations. I have described not only bizarre meteorological phenomena, but the strange things one can do during those events. For most of those seventeen years, I have been looked upon as a fool. I have known for some time now, that if I didn't bake a pretty good chocolate chip cookie or at least generate sufficient income to buy school clothes, my eldest and her teenage friends would have me committed.

"It only happened a couple of times when I was a kid . . ." I would begin. No one believed me, when I described those odd years that the ice froze smooth and clear, like window glass, with no blanket of snow. One could see every grain of sand, every pebble on the bottom of the lake. It was as though time had stopped. We would slide out and study the contours, the depths. Defying gravity, without flying. . . . Stepping out onto a forbidden world of still water. . . . No breeze, no gusts, no ripples to disturb the view. Bright, raw sunlight. . . .

Growing tired, I would lie on my stomach and stare down into that eerie, strange world. Eventually, when I was still enough, quiet enough, the lake trout would slide by, cruising the drop-off for a meal, as usual. At first, I would see only their shadows on the sandy bottom, then an entire silhouette, fins moving. Such fat, healthy fish, oblivious to my presence!

Sometimes we would rig skaters' sails, by tying old bedspreads to poles made of saplings. We would let the wind carry us a half mile out onto the ice. Sometimes we moved so fast that we surprised the fish near the surface or in

Ice

the shallows. They moved sideways, but never seemed to dart. Everything appeared to move slower once the water was cold. The thick ice shifted and "urped." Ice makes a sound like a barking seal when it moves, expanding, contracting. It feels alive and responsive to our presence.

Now, this Christmas day, I plunge my hand into an ice fishing hole made by adolescent boys testing out new equipment. It is a full five inches thick, at least three inches thicker than it looks. We are exhausted from the sheer otherworldliness of walking on water. Darkness forces us to leave the lake, and we pluck our way through the wet and weak spots at the very edge of the water, where earth and ice don't quite merge. Only twelve hours later, the lake is inaccessible, under a foot and a half of snow. A respectful voice whispers, "Mom, it was an honor just to see it."

We don't have a traditional Woodland Indian term for El Nino. It is there, in our oral traditions, in more clumsy terms, such as, "one of those years when Biboon (Winter) came late, and the people were comfortable and lazy." One such year, they were taken by surprise when the lakes froze clear and smooth, with no snow to hide the ice fishermen from the fish. The people were hungry. They set their carved fish-shaped lures beneath their holes in the ice and waited with spears and baited hooks. The bright sun, however, revealed every movement, every leg shifted, every nose scratched, in the shadows cast on the bottom of the lake. The fish were spooked. The people were still hungry. They had thought autumn would last forever and had not yet put away enough food.

The Origins of the First Ice Fishing Shanty

It was at this point that Manaboozhou, (spririt/teacher, part bumbling fool, part successful hero), took time off from ice fishing to construct the first shanty. It was made of intertwined cedar boughs and cast a convoluted shadow that seemed like a good piece of underwater structure to the fish. Unfortunately, the ice was so smooth and slippery that Manaboozhou made quite a ruckus trying to set up the shelter over a likely fishing spot. Once his setup was intact, however, it was merely a waiting game. Although he is not known for his patience, Manaboozhou waited. And he waited. Out of deference to the superior fishing skills of this mysterious spirit man, the people kept their distance from his fishing hole, so as not to spook what would surely be the largest of fish.

Just before dark, Manaboozhou speared a great sturgeon. It was so large that he could not pull it up through the small hole he had driven in the ice. Several men helped to enlarge the hole. Each time Manaboozhou tried to pull up the sturgeon, however, its coarse scale plates caught on the edges of the ice. Efforts continued. The sun disappeared at the close of this shortest of winter days, and there was a span of almost sheer darkness, broken only by starlight. Waiting for an early appearance of the full moon, the men kept cutting the ice. They feared for their safety at the slick, wet precipice, but dared not complain, out of prolonged hunger and respect for their helpful spirit, Manaboozhou. Speed was essential. To lose the injured sturgeon would hurt both man and fish. They remained in awe at their minds' images of the huge fish they had seen through the ice.

The great, round moon finally crested the treetops, flooding the great expanse of the lake and the tense fishermen with much needed light. The fish could see the men, too. Yet the great sturgeon did not put up a fight as it was held on the spear, and the men continued to break the ice. It rolled its eyes and calmly watched the activity, as it was lifted out and dragged across the lake, up the bank, and to the cluster of small homes and waiting families. When stroked lovingly on its flanks and offered tobacco in gratitude for its flesh, the sturgeon merely replied, "You're welcome." That single fish kept the people fed until spring.

Children often ask me, "Are these stories true?" They're all true stories.

Our winter pow wows are smaller and more private than those known to most of the public. They are an opportunity to honor our dead, our leaders, our children, and the changes in the season.

My favorite is the midwinter pow wow. We have not celebrated the winter solstice as many cultures do. Rather, we celebrate about six to eight weeks or so after solstice, when the days have become visibly longer, and the animals and our environment are beginning the most subtle of changes. It is a time of joy and anticipation. We look forward to a lengthening of each workday and a period of gradual warming. It is a matter of outlook, I suppose, although I always feel a sense of loss for the serenity and clean beauty of winter.

Inhaling the Night

At these cold season pow wows, there is a dance that the women do. One only need borrow a shawl to participate. It is the shawl dance, a kind of follow-the-leader game "played" by women of all ages, together, from perhaps the age of fourteen on to the very oldest. Different women take turns being the leader each time. There is a core group who starts it every year. There are whispers, a nod of heads, and then perhaps three women or so will initiate dance from the crowded periphery into the empty center of the dance circle. Within moments, there are at least a dozen of us. Extra shawls have been tucked into boxes for family and friends to borrow. There is rummaging, and the line gets longer.

It is a slow shuffle, very regular and even at first. Then the leader changes her step slightly, and the woman behind her must imitate in the next beat, then the woman behind her, until the line is gently moving and twisting like an elegant, colorful set of dominoes. As the steps change more frequently, there are errors, giggles, a break-up of the *wewebiiminikwaan*, the undulating line. We reassemble, renew, a little practice is all. . . . Soon, the leader restrains herself a bit, and we are all able to follow suit. Now heads are thrown high. We know we are beautiful.

The lodge is hot. It is full of people and food. The previous dancers have been frenzied adolescents at a high-paced beat, filling the room with sweaty mist. Now, the leader shuffles over to the open doorway, and we sinuously dance out into the parking lot, like a sparkling stream disappearing around a bend. The air is cool and refreshing. It lifts the stale heat from our clothing and hair.

We still hear the faint beat of the drum, the strains of the singers from inside the lodge. We continue to dance, enjoying the subtlety of the beat, the freedom from the viewing crowd. We dance in place, eyes to the sky. The song will end soon. The coolness feels so good, that we gulp down the fresh air.

Between the cloudbanks are patches of stars. Holes in the sky, we call them. The darkness and solitude of the outdoors are a welcome break from the business, travel, and preparations of the day.

The music has ended. Giggling, hugs, conversations. Beaming teenagers are congratulated on their dance regalia by the older women they so emulate. Gossip. Good gossip. A gossip born of love and comfort. A feeling that all is well with the world and with family.

It's time to take a quick look to make sure that the kids aren't bothering anybody. It will be time for "giveaway" soon. This is our redistribution system. This is the way our economy used to work. It still does a little bit. There will be flashlights, car batteries, baby clothes, and books for the preschoolers. There will be herbs, fungus, *skwa-toggin, mshkadeehbug, sey-muh*. . . . A twelve-year-old boy with a shiny compact disc in the center of his feather bustle will reach down with an armlet of shimmering porcupine quillwork to grasp at a bundle of sage, perhaps trip on the untied lace of his beaded high top sneaker. . . . These traditions are timeless.

Inhaling the Night

We women trickle in, one by one, chilled. At the door, the sounds, heat, and smells hit each one of us heavily, like a tent flap. Boys chase. Bells jingle. Children squabble. No one inside has missed us. We have been dancing this dance for hundreds of years.

As far as I know, there were only two of us alive in Michigan still making birch bark bitings, although for years Canadian collectors told me about an older lady in the far north who was still making them. Then I started hearing about the lady who made them but was in her eighties. Finally, someone told me that she was gone. One Valentine's Day, I traveled around Lake Nipigon. While there, I demonstrated to some of the Ojibwe and Cree women how to make bark cutouts. Some of the people I spoke to asked if I did bark bitings. It is an art form that is remembered and respected, but no one there knew how or knew of any local individual who still made them. There is so much communication, travel, and intermarriage between the Indian communities of the northern Great Lakes, that word tends to get around about such things. We value the old art forms and want to know who still does what.

Birch Bark Biting

That was back when there were two of us. Then Ron had his eyetooth pulled. The bitings are created only with the eyetooth, and the biter, either right-handed or left- handed, tends to favor one eyetooth over another. Never having gotten the opportunity to demonstrate bitings to any of the interested parties at Lake Nipigon, I found myself the last living soul I knew of still creating this art form. Painfully aware of my own mortality, I began dragging other Indians out into the nearest birch woods. "I don't want the responsibility," I insisted.

Birch bark bitings were originally done strictly for amusement. The designs are traditionally floral and abstract. Pictures of animals are also done, and these are usually at least bilaterally symmetrical. As a child, I saw it done near the small northern Ontario Indian community of Palomar. The bitings were done as a curiosity after dinner, by a couple of older men who peeled the bark directly off of the firewood next to the stove. I was very young and didn't know yet that these things I saw would disappear, so I didn't really pay attention to the details of how the bark was treated. Mostly I remember the joking and cajoling as the designs were held up to the kerosene lamp. One uncle lacked the necessary teeth to make the designs.

Eventually, as an adult, I began to try bark biting as an offshoot of other bark work that I do. It was hard, and it hurt my teeth. One day Ron Paquin, a Native who worked at the Ojibwa Culture Museum in St. Ignace, Michigan, mentioned that he did bitings. He suggested that I try heating the bark over a candle flame to make it more pliable. Although I had known that heat was traditionally used to flatten large sheets of birch bark, it had not occurred to me to try it on such delicate layers. It's tricky. As Ron warned, too much heat destroys the bark.

Today, I make my bitings while I am doing other bark work, utilizing the papery thin layers that peel off but are too thin to fold and cut. I rarely have time to use fresh bark when it is first gathered. Much of my bark work is done during the winter, when the bark is less supple. I trim the bark so that it is symmetrical, because the designs are created strictly by folding, refolding, and planning the bite patterns. I use the pot of hot water on my woodstove to heat the bark. If I am making a particularly complex design, I keep touching parts of the bark to the stove surface. I use the warm water to help pull apart the bitten layers without splitting them. Pressing the unfolded finished pieces onto a hot, cast-iron skillet helps to eliminate fold lines and create a smoother finish for market work.

I don't remember how many years ago I started making the bark bitings. I've gotten better over the years, just because of the hands-on learning experience I've had. It is my absolute favorite traditional art form, because of the surprise element created by the challenge of working with a surface I can't see once it enters my mouth. As with bark cutting, the size, shape, thickness, and texture of each individual piece of bark determines the final product. No two are alike. Birch bark biting is also the single most threatened traditional Woodland Indian art form that I know of. I can teach people how to do the cutouts any time, any place, with paper and scissors. But biting is trickier, and young people think it's "icky," because I put the bark in my mouth

Sometimes when I am out in the woods I pick up pieces of bark that the tree sheds naturally during winter's harsh winds. I make bitings, then lift and release them to flutter away in the breeze. This is how I thank the woodlands for my livelihood. This is my way of leaving a message to future generations that the *Anishnabeg* are still here, that this one small tradition has not yet perished. Sometimes my children find the bitings, years after I have released them. For a few brief moments we admire the tree's gift of a particularly suitable piece of bark, and we wonder at the durability of the medium. Then we send them back to the forest floor. . . . I long to find someone else's, for the security that comes with being part of a mainstream, part of something that is alive and growing, like a culture.

One of our traditional stories tells about a group of siblings who entertained themselves by cutting and biting animal and floral motifs with their mother's basket-making scraps. Preoccupied by the illness of her youngest son, the mother angrily swept the children's "mess" into the fire. Later, her recollection of the bark designs was the only remedy to save the infant's life.

In Ojibwe, *bebookwedagaminh* means "the time of the breaking snowshoe." It is a time somewhere between winter and spring. After the lakes freeze up in late winter, we get fewer clouds, and as the days grow longer, the sun begins to heat up the snowdrifts. The snow compacts and becomes very heavy, wet, and sticky.

The old-style snowshoes were made with rawhide. When dry and cold, it is a very stiff and strong material. It makes for a stiff shoe base and prevents one from sinking into the snow. Wet rawhide, however, stretches and is prone to breaking. It gets mushy and cannot support the weight of a man, especially where the strapping rubs against the wood frame.

Bebookwedagaminh

Bebookwedagaminh. It is a phenomenon that has occurred every year without fail. The Ojibwe break their snowshoes. We try oiling them, but the melting snow seeps into the rawhide. We try starting out the day by facing to the east and offering tobacco. We ask the spirit keepers of the eastern door to lower the temperature so as to protect the rawhide on our snowshoes, but there is no guarantee. Sometimes they listen, and sometimes they don't.

We try asking old Biboon (Winter) to retreat to his home in the far north, but he is stubborn. He doesn't always listen. He obstinately throws his heavy, wet blanket upon the earth. Biboon skulks and waits around corners.

Biboon seems to leave no footprints. He moves with the cold air. He does not need snowshoes. Consequently, he has no sympathy for the *Anishnabeg*, the earth-bound people with small, narrow feet who trudge through his snow. So Ojibwe tradition has taught us to take care of our snowshoes, to carry extra rawhide, to teach our children how to twist, weave, and tie together wood and leather.

Traditionally, the *Anishnabeg* have hung dreamcatchers above the cradleboards and beds of babies and sleeping children. Often, they are hung in a window. The sinew webbing, stitched to a red willow frame, is used to catch "bad" dreams, and only good dreams are allowed to slip through the small hole in the center. Usually, a single bead is worked into the webbing, to demonstrate the concept of a bad dream being caught and concentrated. Children are protected, as the bad ideas are carried down a trailing tail of ribbon or sinew to a single feather. Light as a feather, the bad thoughts are carried skyward and are transformed into sweet dreams.

It's a great idea. We all feel the need to protect babies. They're innocent and sweet. So dreamcatchers have been quite a marketable concept over the years. They've taken on every form, shape, and combination of beads and feathers imaginable. I see them hanging from Christmas trees, rearview mirrors, and necklaces. I don't usually mind too much as long as they are not made in Third World sweatshops (or New World sweatshops, for that matter).

Dreamcatchers

But dreamcatchers are more than mere tourist art to most Native people, and I hate to see important traditions become buried in stereotypes. In practical terms, dreamcatchers were nice, sturdy, round, smooth, *safe* things for babies to bat around on the roll bars of their cradleboards and portable seats, while their moms were busy doing something else. Today, they subtly remind Native children that they belong to cultural traditions that are unique and attractive, even if far from mainstream. And they are *pretty*. That's worth something in any culture. That's why they were often used as decorations on dance clothing long ago, or were even dangled from trees outside of a wigwam, catching the breezes.

Sometimes dreamcatchers are used as teaching tools. The first time my eldest was taught to make dreamcatchers by an aunt, she was taught something else much more important: to thank the tree. I remember sticking my head out the window, before they reached the door, upon their return from their foraging trip, "Did you remember to thank the tree?" I was consciously aware of the absurdity of the question a moment after it left my lips. ("There aren't that many people who wouldn't think I am crazy. . . ." I remember thinking.)

"Yee-eesss!" The respondent was obviously annoyed that I questioned her exercise of protocol. Wild tobacco, or *sey-muh*, had been deposited at the base of the tree from which the necessary branches had been nipped. This was done to remind the harvester not to take too much from one spot, and to recognize each and every plant as a valuable resource. This was done to remind the child that she was a part of a vast circle of life, a *valuable* part of that cycle, one with privileges and responsibilities.

Few people realize the ancient and important survival skills that we share with our children by teaching them how to make dreamcatchers. This is an example of a toy being used to teach life skills: knowing where, when, and how to obtain the right wood and how to bend it, knowing how to obtain and prepare the twines, rawhide, oils, and finishes . . . these are the real secrets and the real stories behind dreamcatchers. If we can make a dreamcatcher, we can frame up and weave almost anything, including snowshoes, fishing weirs, tools, and even small buildings.

Although they have become almost a cliché in the modern marketplace, dreamcatchers are really a cultural symbol of common sense and survival skills. I value them as ornaments, but I respect them as something greater, especially when I'm knee deep in the snow, or as I watch a baby develop its motor skills, or as I watch an adult spend time with a younger person.

It is said that, in the old times, in the earliest days of ice-out, at the tail end of winter, people sometimes became sick from not eating enough fruits and vegetables. This often happened to those who could not or did not put away enough rice, nuts, and dried fruits. The remedy for this illness was thought to be the fresh liver of a small mouth bass.

One year a particular family was suffering greatly from hunger and weakness. Malnourished, they could scarcely fend for themselves. The man of the household continually berated his wife and daughters for their laziness and failure to put away enough food. Although whenever others had visited his household, he had set out wasteful quantities of fruits and rice to im- press his guests and preserve the honor he perceived they would bestow upon him. He, himself, had been lazy in his commitment to put away stores of meat, fish, and wood. In fact, there were those in the community who suspected that the man's hard-working wife and daughters would have been even more productive, had they not spent so much time frozen in fear of the man's erratic temper. Still others speculated that the family would, indeed, have survived the long cold season in greater health had the man not traded away several *waushkiishuk* (thirty-pound bags) of rice in exchange for an elaborate, multistranded bear claw necklace. Some even joked about the irony of such a symbol of hunting prowess and leadership hanging about the chest of such a lazy, miserable wife beater.

The man did occasionally drag himself away from his wife's fire at midday to walk to the homes of his neighbors, hinting at his need for vegetables or, even better yet, a fresh bass liver—not for himself, of course, but for the benefit of his

In Pursuit of Shiigun, the Bass

family. After all, he insisted, he would himself die first, before denying his loved ones a bite of nourishment.

After making the rounds among his neighbors for a few weeks, gobbling up the proceeds of his labor before reaching his own wigwam, he ran out of neighbors . . . and options. Knowing full well that his kinsmen would look down upon him for letting his wife and children perish, he resolved himself to obtain the liver of a small mouth bass. This would be no small task, as the bass was known to be elusive during this particular season. Shiigun, the bass, was still hiding in the deep waters, only beginning to scout out his spawning grounds in the rocky shallows of inlets at the water's edge. Weeks of lengthening, cloudless days and clear, cold nights made for uncertain ice. It was this weakened ice at the edges of the lakes that the man would have to traverse to get to the drop-offs most likely to yield a bass.

Rising at his usual late hour, the man spent the first few days of effort motionless and well within the confines of the safest ice structures of a shallow cove. Watchful neighbors conjectured that he would put out the visual affect of effort at best, before someone would eventually step in and rescue his family. Others even hoped that the *michigaamigag,* the underwater spirits, would entice him out onto thinner ice.

However, it was Shiigun himself who lured the poor, lazy soul to the drop-off at the edge of the ice. Time after time, he leaped out of the water, showing himself to the man. (This enticement took no small effort on the part of the fish, as even small mouth bass stay sluggish if the water is too cold.) Eventually, the man crept out on his belly, to the edge of the ice, to observe the aggravating fish. This entertained his voyeuristic neighbors to no small extent.

Now, this man gave up on his spear and slid back to shore to fetch the nets his wife and daughters had carefully woven and mended over the years (although this is man's work). Time and time again, the bass avoided the fine threads of the net as the man lay on his belly, observing. Time and time again, the bass came close, only to dodge away, to slip through, to tease, to consternate, to confound the desperate and inept fisherman.

Mumbling to himself about the poor net-mending skills of his female charges, the man unwound the long bear claw necklace from his own neck. He hastily intertwined its sharp claws with the strands of the net. "Slip through this!" he hissed, and he rolled back to shore to sip pine needle tea at his wife's fire, leaving the lethal trap untended through the rest of that day, that night, and well into the next day.

Upon his eventual return to the claw-strewn net, the man angrily hoped for the demise of old Shiigun himself. Instead, he found several of Shiigun's wives and daughters, fat with eggs, entangled in the nets. Cruelly, he twisted the fibers, until the sharp claws pierced the bodies of the female bass. Blood and roe floated up to the edges of the ice as he lifted the nets out of the open water. Safely on shore, he cut open the fish and ate the fresh livers himself before returning home. As he handed the fish to his wife to clean and cook, he explained that he needed to heal himself so that he could adequately provide for his useless family.

The next day, the man did not go back out onto the thinning ice. More days passed, and the ice grew thinner. Neighbors watched, hopeful that the man would venture out one more time onto the dangerous ice. In the end, however, it was not the man who went out. It was his wife and daughters. Rising long before their man was accustomed to do, they went unnoticed by the other people of the village.

It was an angry and vengeful Shiigun who waited for them at the edge of the thin ice, where the water was deep. Upon seeing their shadows crawling over the ice, he rose to the surface, accompanied by his companions, the *michigaamigag*. As the creatures lifted themselves up from below, a gust of southerly wind swept up, and the thin layer of ice upon which the women lay was gone. . . . There are those among those watchful neighbors who looked up in time and caught the spectacle.

It is said that those drowned women became the Shiigun-kwe,

In Pursuit of Shiigun, the Bass

the Bass Sisters, the green-scaled women who live under the water with Shiigun, the great bass. They no longer go hungry, and he never uses a harsh word against them. They are better off, say the neighbors. Some believe that it is the Bass Sisters who lure fishermen to join them under the surface of the water, in one attempt after another to take revenge upon their abuser. Once a fisherman joins them, he can never return to his own wife and children. However, the women were never able to lure in the lazy man who was responsible for their deaths. He survived alone in a cold and dirty wigwam. In that particular village, a bear claw came to symbolize cruelty and abuse against women and children.

Rumor has it that this was the origin of hate among the *Anishnabeg*, or Ojibwe. Laziness lent itself to blame and anger, exacerbated by an endless cycle of revenge.

Today, each spring, we go to the edge of the water to sing to that enormous, confounding bass and his spirit companions. The men in their bear claw necklaces prevail upon their guardians to send them strength to nurture their women and children and to heal the hurt and indifferences of past generations. Women shake the turtle shell rattles and dip their knees in time to the music. The ice breaks up on the shore, and the water wears it into smooth boulders, then pebbles, then specks of ice the size of beads, riding the cresting waves against the shore. And we hear them rattling, *shiishii . . . shiishii . . . shiishiigohnan.* . . . The men sing to the south wind, and the ice pellets, with their echoes of ancient rattles, are gone.

In our imaginations there are, in every rock outcropping, cannibalistic monsters called *wiindigoog*. They come from the west, are fast runners with huge appetites, and can be called up by any gust of wind. Periodically, and with little warning, they gobble up a lone villager.

It is said that, in a particular village, a foolish man challenged one of the *wiindigoog* to a race. There was wagering upon the outcome. If the man won, the *wiindigoog* would stay away from the village and never eat any of its residents again. Were he to lose, that particular *wiindigo* would gobble up every man, woman, and child in the village.

The outcome was predictable. No man had ever been able to run faster than the *wiindigoog*, faster than the wind itself. No man would ever be able to run faster than a giant, supernatural being. And that is what happened. The man lost the race. So it came to be, that there was a village where only the children had been able to outrun that terrible *wiindigo*. There was only one surviving adult. This was wise old Nokomis, the grandmother, who soothed, hid, and fed each of these weary children as they ran from sunrise to sunset.

Chiibii Tag

Now, in our imaginations, as the grownups are busy at their work and play, we become the dwellers of that village of children running, running, running nonstop. A few of the larger boys always volunteer to become the *wiindigoog,* and the rest of us run for our lives. If we are caught, we are "*chiibii*-ed," we are frozen in place, frozen in fear, like ghosts. Usually, the oldest child plays the part of Nokom, our Grandmother. The only way we can be freed is if Nokom "feeds" us, or touches us. The only way we can rest is by touching Nokom. This can be difficult since Nokomis is busy running around freeing all the *chiibiig,* the ghosts. Having other children attached to her can slow her down considerably, and she may opt to push her children away after a while. If a child breaks touch with Nokom, then that child can be tagged by a *wiindigo,* so the monsters may chase Grandmother herself.

Eventually, the *wiindigoog* might grow tired of the chase, or the children might all be frozen and eaten. Or, the whole group may decide to let the sun set and continue the game tomorrow. All it really takes to call up the spirits is a large, dark rock or a gust of warm wind. . . .

*S*iisagwad. The first time I saw this word in written form, I was surprised. Visually, it is a homely word. But to the experienced ear, it is music. Siiiiisagwad. It is onomatopoeia, a word that imitates the sound that it describes. It is the sound that the wind makes in the trees. Siiiiiiiiiisagwaaaad. Spoken from the lungs, it is whispered with reverence.

As a toddler, I can remember early one morning climbing into bed with my uncle and aunt. It must not have been a particularly cold morning, because I did not burrow deeply under the covers as I usually did when I snuggled into the middle, usually to the objection of siblings, parents, or whomever I inflicted my cold toes upon. I sat up to chatter that morning, but was quickly shushed: *"K'piiisssandan!"*

Siisagwad

"Listen! Listen to it. Siiiiiisssagwad. It's different this morning."

During the warm spring night, the sap had risen into the branches of the pines. They no longer reached skyward like branches of tightly closed, chilly winter trees. Heavy now, the branches were down at the height of the window, their needle clusters open wide, grasping at tufts of wind that happened by. It was the sound of renewal, of a new growing season. The wind had lost its cold winter howl, and it was replaced by a slower, softer, fuller sound.

The *siisagwad* crept into the crack of the open window and swept me back out with it, in and out among the trunks and branches of the familiar pines. I danced from branch tip to branch tip with the pine squirrels in the dim light of the brightening morning. Then I glided back inside on the *siisagwad*, to the warm bed, the loving hands of big people.

The house had its own soft thumping sounds. I slid off of the bed and flowed out to the kitchen, following the welcome morning sounds of the refrigerator door and the crackling of a pack of saltines being opened by young hands. The sound of the wind, I temporarily took for granted.

We call it *wiingush,* the sacred plant of the north. Sweet-grass. It is so special, so sacred, that we have no tales about its origin. No one dare approach the subject. When the children play with it as we pick it, we tell them in hushed tones not to trample it, to treat it with respect. "You are braiding the hair of our Mother Earth. It does not grow all over her body, only in a few special places." So we travel miles, even days, to harvest the sturdiest and sweetest smelling of all wild grasses.

We use sweetgrass to make baskets and to trim birch bark and porcupine quillwork. It is a wrong against our people and our culture to sell it. But, as artists and basket makers, we have a gift. We are part of a tradition of specialization that is essential to all cultures. We make beauty, and we share it. We are among the few who are al-lowed to take, transform, and utilize this sa-cred plant.

Charlie's Bundle

I have been told that, in the old days, sweetgrass baskets were used to filter drink-ing water. Even today, it is burned to ease the symptoms of migraine headaches. It is smudged each morning by some, in order to face the oncoming day's responsibilities. It is part of *kiniginig,* a special tobacco mixture. We protect it. We cure and store it with the utmost care. We touch it with reverence. And we *never* waste a bit of it. Even the tiniest scraps are prayed over when they are burned.

The locations are secret, the picking, processing, curing, and sharing of it so laden with tradition that it feels overwhelming. Now, in this heat, fighting off the bugs, the eerie calls of the watchful ravens, the overhead threats of the Thunderbirds, echoed by an awestruck three-year-old . . . these feelings are compounded by the fact that it is profoundly backbreaking and physically exhausting to harvest. It must be picked one blade at a time, with two hands. With each blade I stand up straight again, to clean it, to rest my back. Then I carefully remove and instantly replant any accidentally pulled roots.

I begin to make a mental list of elders and those less able with whom I will share this sacred, fragrant plant. This is a tradition that carries on from the very first time I was taken here . . . to bring *wiingush* to the older people, the basket makers, the ones with the knowledge and the skills, the dying language. . . . Along with this precious secret, and the mysteries that surround it, come responsibilities.

My oldest child is picking quietly, tiptoeing gently. Tonight I will suggest to her that she remove from her hard-earned bundle enough sweetgrass to share. But her thoughts are already moving in the right direction, as she begins to suggest names on her own. I swell with pride. I am proud of the job I have done. I have passed on reverence to one with whom I have shared the secret of the location. I am a good mom, and she is an equally good daughter.

After I tell her that it is time to wrap and put away our own supply for the year, I nurse the baby in the tall, fragrant grass. We mutually decide that we will now pick a separate bundle for Charlie. We will not cure it, but will express mail it to him in its pure state, so as not to rob him of that pleasure, that tradition. Surely, it has been many years since he has had that opportunity.

We carefully review the procedure for curing the sweetgrass, step by step, so that we can share it with him. It will be her job to write it down for him. I know she knows the information by heart now. With this last contrived lesson, I have reviewed the procedure with her one more time. She's watched and helped every year for as long as she can remember. But now, I am sure, the traditional knowledge is safely bundled up inside of her.

Charlie's bundle keeps getting bigger. There is an issue of pride, making sure he isn't cheated of his heritage, his tradition,

Charlie's Bundle

his honor. The bundle grows far larger than it would have been had we pulled it out of our own precious store. We work with a renewed energy that belies the early hour of rising, hours of driving, the heat, the strained effort of bringing children through the roughest of trails. With every blade of grass, we think of Charlie—his soft voice, his patience, his shared knowledge, his patient wife. My little girl takes off her shirt and lovingly wraps the bundle, weaving through the woods, over the deadfalls we leave in place to hide the trail. As she stares at me, exhausted, out the tailgate of the car, I sweep away our footprints. Think of me on mother's day, Charlie.

It was a ritual that we had grown used to, we and our cousins. The afternoons at the home of my grandmother's brother, Great Uncle Leonard, a small, rough shack by the side of the lake, smelling of molasses cookies. We had to earn those cookies first, as audience and actors, in an event of traditional Ojibwe theater/school/teaching lodge/family entertainment. We gathered in a semicircle, scuffling, making "dibs" on the few chairs. Then, the magic . . . the masks . . . the transformations. . . .

Are you Manaboozhou (Nanabush)? *Kaah!* Are you Chiibiaboozhou, the dead brother? *Kaah, kaah!* Are you a spirit by any other name? *Kaah, kaah, kaah!* Then, who are you? *Indizhnikaash Chii Mukwah, I am a big bear!* A thin old man in a flannel shirt, he removed the simple, folded birch bark mask. Yet there he was, as much a bear as one would ever see, manipulating our imaginations.

Manaboozhou and the Ducks

Oh, I simply must tell you what happened to me, late one fall, when I'd found the perfect hollow log within which to stuff my fat and healthy, big, hairy self. The fangs were fairly gleaming . . . the belly round and brown. It had been a good year for fattening up for hibernation. The blueberries were sparse, but the cranberries were good. I'd eaten many grubs and minnows. I'd ventured into a rocky shallow and had found many whitefish who had moved in with the advent of cold weather. Oh, I was fat!

I'd backed into the perfect hollow log, bum first, as is my way. It was a good, sturdy, long hollow maple, with but one large knothole, and that was way up on a long branch sticking out. No cold winter breezes to bother me. I was a happy bear. I had just snuggled in and was just barely asleep, when it happened—that Manaboozhou, lazy, bumbling fool, he surprised me!

How? How?

Let me explain. . . . All of the animals were fattening up for the winter. The Anishnaabeg *were gathering and storing all sorts of foods—berries, dried roots, meats, and fish. Things were sometimes ready for such a short period of time that everyone had to work exhaustingly long hours harvesting. The* Anishnabeg *worked especially hard gathering wild rice, hundreds of pounds of it. They pounded it into the canoes and took it to shore, where other teams of workers parched it, winnowed it, and wrapped and packed it away for lean times. They also harvested the ducks and water birds that came to fatten up on the rice. Everyone was busy, except that fool, Manaboozhou. . . . Although he was half human, he often relied upon the spirit half of his ancestry to get by. He rarely put up enough stores for winter.*

He whiled away his time on the shores of the potholes teasing the ducks. He knew that they couldn't resist a tidbit of fish, so he offered them a bit of tough, tanned lake trout skin. Each time it would pass through the duck, undigested. Gleefully, he would search for that same piece of leather in the shallows and toss it to another duck. Even after weeks and weeks of this game, he never tired of it. However, as the water grew colder, especially in the shallower ponds, he disliked wading in after his tidbit of leather duck bait.

Now, he had a brainstorm of sorts. Why not tie that piece of trout leather onto a string, so he could simply pull it out of the water when the duck was done with it? He fashioned a tightly woven string out of basswood fibers. It was a beautiful string, some say, as it is Manaboozhou, fool that he is, who invented the stuff and taught the rest of us how to make it.

Chii Mukwah took a deep breath and scratched his big belly with a sharp, curved claw. . . . *Oh, and he was a fool, that Manaboozhou, for he did not think ahead that each duck would be somewhere along that string, between his hand on one end and the bait on the other. The first duck on the string was funny, the second hilarious. Now, he knew, his superior intellect had allowed him to gather all the duck meat he would need to dry and freeze for winter, all without the planning and labor of mere men and other beasts of the north. So, with a jerk of the string, it was time to haul in his catch.*

Ah, but the jerk of a string on the sensitive bills and backsides of all those ducks sent them up at once, in a fluttering and flapping of wings, feet, and water. The entire flock was momentarily airbound, with the fool still holding the string, rising above the treetops. "They cannot support my weight for long," thought Manaboozhou. "They will come back to earth." They pulled the fool up beyond that hill there! Our eyes followed Uncle's thin finger, as it pointed out the window, at a crest across the bay.

You've seen me over there, hunting for fish remains. Where do you think I'd planned to winter over? Well, right in that hollow on the other side of that hill, out of the wind. And, well, where do you think that idiot lost his hold on that string full of ducks? Right above my winter house, I say! The big fellow dropped like a rock. He found that very knothole in that very branch sticking up from my log. The force of his fall was so great, that it wedged him straight down into the main body of the log, directly behind me, right on top of my long, beautiful tail!

How was I supposed to know who it was in there with me? I'd been asleep. Besides, if I'd known that it was that bumbling Manaboozhou, I'd have been just as scared as if it was a wildcat. . . . I did what any self-respecting bear would do—I growled. Next thing I knew, he was shrieking, "Did you hear that? There's a horrible beast in here with us! We've got to get out of here!" So I did what any self-respecting bear would do—I growled again. He shrieked again. And he started pushing on my behind, trying to stuff me back out of my nice, tight log, but I didn't want to go! So I growled again. And the fool shrieked again. It was awful!

I started to claw my way right out of that comfy log, no matter how fat I still was. "Don't leave me here alone with it!" a voice behind me called out. The next thing I knew, that fool had both hands clamped around my tail. I tugged, and I tugged, and I popped out of that log, but the fool was stuck in there behind me. It happened so fast, I was halfway over the hill before I noticed that he still had my long, beautiful tail in his hands. That's why I've hardly any tail left at all. Just like a poor little rabbit. It's so embarrassing!

Speaking of rabbits, that fool Manaboozhou was so scared and panicked that he'd forgotten that he could change himself into any kind of creature he wanted. When he finally quit screaming, "Don't leave me!" he changed himself into a little rabbit and hopped right out of that hollow log. He left my poor tail in there, too. This summer, you go look in that hollow log over beyond that hill. See if you don't still find a bit of my fur there. . . .

All that, and cookies, too.

North and west of our island, the other islands stretch around the cape of Gargantua, along the northeast shore of Lake Superior. The small islands are interspersed with shoals of volcanic rock, called "frying pans," so close under the surface that the water appears to froth like hot fat with the slightest swell or wave. This is a deadly, open cape of downwind shoreline exposed to the longest unbroken stretch of open water on Lake Superior. It is traversable by canoe, due to the chain of islands and shoals. The open route is sinuous and unexpected. At times, the water is 30 meters deep an arm's length from the rocky shore, and the safer looking water farther out is actually the most dangerous. Uncle Dick taught the safest route to my husband and me. Along with the local Indian fishermen, we have it memorized. Its modern name is the "Tugboat Channel," as it is deep enough for a large fishing tug or even a cabin cruiser.

The Devil's Chair

Traversing the Tugboat Channel was a danger that reaped incredible rewards for my Native ancestors. The water-worn, ragged edges of the earth have been scoured clean by thousands of years of activity by the great inland sea. Exposed were raw copper, volcanic glass, high-quality chert for arrowheads, pipestone, and red ochre—all valuable trade commodities. As well, the underwater structure provided for excellent fishing, before the opening up of the Great Lakes to the Saint Lawrence Seaway and foreign aquatic species, and before large-scale commercial overfishing decimated the sturgeon and trout populations. Even my grandmother pilgrimaged regularly to the area, using early-twentieth-century outboard motor power, no doubt equal in foolhardiness to traversing miles of coastline by canoe.

At the northern mouth of the Tugboat Channel, Manaboozhou rests in the water, looking out over the length of this
largest of freshwater lakes in the world. Picking up cues from
the Native population, early voyageurs, in great canoes laden
with furs to and from the Michipicoten trading post to the
north, left offerings at the great rock outcropping. Some time in
history, some one misconstrued the word "sitting" for "chair."
We are wont to blame the Jesuits. For some reason, everything
that made reference to the competing, non-Christian Ojibwe
belief system was referred to as "the Devil's. . . ." *The Devil's
Chair. The Devil's Frying Pan. The Devil's Warehouse.* The Devil's
this, the Devil's that. The Devil's Children. For us, it gets kind
of old. . . .

Manaboozhou is far from a devil. Half spirit and half human,
he is a powerful teacher. He is also a bumbling fool, with a rep-
utation for both working hard and being lazy. He is humorous
and much loved. We have countless stories about him. We say
that, the nice thing about being Indian is, we don't learn by our
own mistakes—we have Manaboozhou to do it for us.

Once Manaboozhou sat next to his campfire on a hill over-
looking the great lake. Two streams led away in opposite direc-
tions from the peak of the hill. One wound slightly to the
south, the other slightly to the north. Both drained into the big
lake. Today, both remain dammed up by beavers, forming deep
and sinuous pike lakes, before seeping under long dams into
Lake Superior.

Far beneath him, Manaboozhou saw about fifteen ducks
feasting together in the shallows. Fifteen fat ducks, and one
loon. Now, a duck usually does not think by itself. It often
takes many ducks to have a complete thought. If one sees three
ducks drinking, one thinks, "Oh, one of them must be thirsty."
So it was, that Manaboozhou knew that he did not need to
shout, to risk startling the ducks. He needed only to whisper, to
catch the attention of one or two of those ducks, to lure the
whole bunch of them up the hill. (The loon did not matter, as
they are not good eating.) To chase a bunch of ducks around a

big lake down there in the rocky shallows would be a lot of work. To woo them up to his cooking fire would be a stroke of genius. . . .

"Pssssss. . . . Hey! *Kipiiiiiisssssssandan, kipiiiiisssssssandanawan* . . ." He smiled. His movements were kept restrained. He motioned only with his head. "Listen up! I've got something to share with you."

"Come on up, all of you. I've got something to share. I've got a great new song and dance I want to teach you folks." He pointed with his bottom lip, keeping his hands in his pockets, trying to look unobtrusive. "Over here, up on top of the hill. You're gonna love this!"

Managing to get the attention of one of the ducks closest to shore, the spirit man lured the whole bunch of ducks up the hill, slowly, patiently muttering and waddling their way to the top, in a long line, with the single loon at the end. Ah, a line. Perfect. This would be a line dance. Follow the leader.

"Stay in that line, you ducks. Perfect." He began to sway slightly, moving in a circle about the fire pit, gently at first, so as not to startle the ducks.

"This song does not need a drum," said Manaboozhou, placing his palm to his thigh in a gentle rhythm. (He wanted to keep his hands free.) "This is a dance that is done to the *siisagwad,* the sound of the wind in the trees, to the *weweyaashigaw,* the music of the waves lapping at the beach. Do you hear those sounds? No? Better to listen to them with your eyes shut. You know your way around the circle now. . . . These sounds are beautiful and magical. No peeking. If you peek, your eyes will turn red, and the other ducks won't like you much."

Now Manaboozhou began to pick up the pace. The flapping of the ducks' feet made quite a racket. A delicious racket. Manaboozhou began to hum a little, softly . . . then louder, to cover up his sounds. Every few beats, he reached behind him and strangled the ducks, one by one, tossing them into a pile, off to the side of the cooking fire. He sang out a big "Heya!" each time, to cover up the thump of a nice, fat duck landing on the pile.

The Devil's Chair

Now, if there is any water bird more sociable than a duck, it is a loon. A loon is a snoop. A loon will always call out and look over its shoulder at the other loons, to keep track of things. So it was with this loon. Constantly interrupting the song to ask what was going on, constantly being shushed by Manaboozhou, Loon couldn't stand it anymore. He opened his eyes and peeked. To this day, Loon's eyes are red . . . Ducks avoid him.

"He's killing us! He wants to eat us!" Loon cried out.

The remaining ducks scattered.

"Hey! That was rude! I wasn't going to eat you. You taste terrible!" Manaboozhou chastised the loon. "Go ahead, fly off, all of you. I've got plenty to eat already."

Now, plucking ducks is a lot of work. The feathers are pulled out dry, and then the skin is singed over hot coals to remove the finest "hairy" feathers that remain. An old way to cook ducks on an open fire was to leave the feet intact as handles, and to stuff the body cavities with cattail roots and wild onions, before inserting the ducks into a bed of slow coals. All of those duck feet handles sticking out in a circle around the roasting coals was a beautiful sight.

Worn out from all of his work, Manaboozhou laid down next to the fire, watching the embers glow. As his eyelids began to droop from the dry heat, he turned his backside to the fire, to warm it up. Aware that the fatty ducks needed to be watched closely, Manaboozhou instructed his backside to watch the fire for him. He dozed off. . . .

Now, a crow is a bird that does not go to sleep early. A man can easily fall asleep to the sound of crows. So it was with Manaboozhou. Crow and Raven, two birds who do not discriminate, who will eat anything, live or dead, raw or cooked, saw an opportunity for themselves. And, they called in their relations. As Manaboozhou slept, he was robbed. The bones were picked clean and tossed into the fire to burn. As a final joke, Crow and Raven stuck the empty duck feet back in a circle all around the edge of the fire pit.

When he woke up, Manaboozhou rolled over and smacked his lips. He salivated at the thought of one, plump, juicy duck after another. He hefted at the pair of feet closest to him, only to rock backward with the unnecessary effort, as there was no duck attached to the feet. One after another, he pulled out the empty pairs of duck feet, shocked and disappointed.

At no time did it occur to him that he might have been robbed. "Fool!" He turned around and screamed at his own backside. "You didn't watch the fire! You let my ducks burn up to a crisp!" He could smell the charred bones now.

So now Manaboozhou invented a new dance, the "try to kick yourself in the butt dance." Fumbling among the scramble of ducks' feet and the burning logs that radiated out from the fire pit, he circumnavigated the circle of hot stones and dying embers . . . once. . . . then twice . . . then a third time. . . . The fourth time is always a winner. Persistence would pay off. Manaboozhou leapt and twisted in midair, reaching for his own rear end with his foot. He landed at the edge of the hot coals before completing the kick. The moccasined foot struck a burning log just right, sending it into the air. Before he knew it, Manaboozhou's rear end was on fire.

Screeching from the pain, like a misplaced downdraft howling through a steep mountain streambed, the fool lurched from his campsite and spun to the north. With one spring, he was far enough downhill to catch a substantial flow in the streambed, where he squatted over that trickle of water in the hopes of putting out the fire. To this day, the plants that grow along the streamside, like coachmen's whips and red willows, are bright red and yellow from the trail of licking flames that he left behind him as he worked his way downhill to the great lake. There, below the beaver dam, are the huge skid marks, preserved in stone.

Tssssssssssssttt . . ."Ah!" There he sits, to this day. By canoe or boat, from the north, one can clearly see him slumped there, his large buffoon feet sticking up askance, his great knuckles protruding from the water, his head thrown back in great relief. There he will rest as long as the lake will let him. Devil, indeed!

The rock outcropping at Cape Gargantua, on the shores of Lake Superior, known as the Devil's Chair, has many stories to go along with it. There are those who say that the spirit, Nanabush, made a habit of regularly jumping across Lake Superior the long way, from west to east. It was along this cape that he rested, panting, looking back across the lake at his great accomplishment.

Nanabush, being half spirit, indeed, accomplished a great many amazing things that no human could do. But his mother was human, and this human side of the spirit left him prone to human error and foibles. No matter how great his feats, and no matter how difficult they may have been to him at the time of their accomplishment, no matter how many false starts and mistakes he made, Nanabush was subject to bravado and exaggeration. Like most braggarts, he selected his audiences carefully and did not commit his exploits to permanent record, lest he offend the parties who witnessed the actual event or whom he claimed to have outwitted or overcome.

Fine Weather for Painting

Only a few meters from the spot where the great lake jumper consistently landed and reposed was an island surrounded by rocky shoals. It was a favorite spot of his to visit, upon resting up from the considerable effort of the long leap. Exposed on the rocky lake side of the island was a great outcropping of chert, from which he would sometimes whack loose a "mother stone," or core piece of stone to carry away for making arrow and spear heads at a later time.

Some years, when the water level of the lake dipped very low, or when the lake was in seiche (its contents sloshed over to the far shore, as though it were a large bowl of water being tilted), a great flat of smooth, exposed rock lay before him for several acres. Nanabush looked upon this as an opportunity. He always had a bit of red ochre tucked into the folds of his soft skin shirt, because he often made a mudpack of it to keep mosquitoes and flies off of his face and ears.

He had just finished eating a large sturgeon and knew where he had left its springy, cartilaginous spinal cord. In a very short time, he had made himself a pot of sticky paint.

Lapsing into utter, uncontrolled vanity, Nanabush decided that it would be an absolute shame for his exploits to go un-recorded for posterity. This was, after all, a rather remote and rugged area of the coastline, and no one of significance would notice if he embellished the tales of his adventures just a little bit, just for the sake of a good story . . . just to keep up the mo-mentum, just to make things interesting, to add to the sus-pense. . . . After all, people expected a great deal from him. He owed it to the *Anishnabeg* to be their hero. These stories *had* to be *good*.

It was a fine day for painting. The sun warmed the rocks. The thunderbirds were far from that place, so the water was as calm as it could possibly be. He could see his own reflection in it, as he painted away. Perhaps his reflection was distorted by the surface of the lake, or by his own imagination, but in Nanabush's mind, he became bigger and bigger, bolder and bolder. . . .

There are those who say that the stories that Nanabush de-picted in paint became overblown to the point of absurdity. He had thrown away all caution about offending the other spirits and painted himself as the witty one, the strong one, the supe-rior one, in every way imaginable. There could be no spirit who might pass by that stone shelf unoffended, were the images to remain intact and clear forever.

Calm as it was, the weather on Lake Superior is completely unreliable. Realizing that they had neglected this stretch of shoreline for several days, the thunderbirds, wings out-stretched, made a quiet and easy scan of the islands. Spying that fool Nanabush, they decided to move in and see what kind of mischief he was up to. What was he hunching over? They silently glided in even closer.

Heh, heh. Cute story about those crows. Ar, ar, ar! Great story about that bear. Yeah, I could see a bear doing something dumb like that. . . . The wolves . . . yup, ignorant and easy to fool, aren't they?

Hey! Wait a minute! That is *not* funny! Have you ever seen an eagle with a big, crooked beak like that? That is *rude!*

And so their thoughts inflamed them. The thunderbirds began beating their wings in anger, somewhat restrained at first, but then increasing in intensity, as they witnessed one offensive exploit after another painted in bright red on the stone shelf below. Nanabush claimed to have made fools of them over and over. He'd gone from stretching the truth to downright fabrication.

Now their wings were beating with ferocity. The winds whipped up out of nowhere, as they are known to do on Lake Superior. The sky darkened. The heavy raindrops pounded the shoreline with the intent of scouring away the offending stories before the cartilage paint had a chance to cure in the sun, before the fabrications were set into the stone with permanent pigment . . . so that no future generations would mistake them for fact rather than fiction.

This is how those stories and images became blurred and incomplete. They are still there. When the water is low, or the lake is as still as stone, I like to go there and piece them together. I can see the otters, the great fishes, and many thunderbirds among the self-portraits of Nanabush himself. If only he had not been so vain, so that the thunderbirds would have allowed him to leave intact something not too far from the real truth. Sometimes, when I think that I am making some sense of it all, when I can clearly see the thunderbirds foolishly tumbling from the sky after being fooled by Nanabush, I feel the chill of an unexpected gust of wind.

I grew up hearing many stories about Niimik Niigik. His name means Niimik the Otter. It doesn't pack much of a punch in English, but in Ojibwe, it is hysterically funny. He comes across much the same as the hand puppet characters White Fang and Black Tooth that were invented by the TV personality Soupy Sales. Niimik is, at first glance, not especially bright. As a story progresses, however, he is genuinely on top of things.

I observe Niimik Niigik today, with the eyes of an adult, so I put him and his behaviors into a light that I could not have put him into as a child. Every time I see an otter, he makes more and more sense to me. He does not mature with age and experience . . . I do. Niimik's

Niimik Niigik

name is a homonym for dance, and it makes sense to me. He is quite a dancer.

Niimik Niigik lives with his brothers in a small inland lake close to my house. There are no homes on the lake, except for an old beaver house that was abandoned some years ago. The boys have taken it over as their home. Sometimes when I am in the canoe, they noisily arrive into the basin I am fishing. I hear them before I see them, as they purr in turn to one another, as though they are discussing the day's foraging. When they see me, they talk to one another, heads turning this way and that, as though I am not there. When I speak, they all hush for a moment, turning their tiny ears to me.

Niimik is the bravest. He swims up close, within two or three meters of the canoe, and propels himself up two-thirds of the way out of the water, to get a good, serious look. If there are fish on the stringer, I must pull them into the canoe, or the hard, fast tug will pull the entire canoe backwards. No, Niimik, you cannot have my dinner! The three of them dip and dive, calmly crunching away on crustaceans as they observe until they are bored, leaving me in a sort of stroll-swim as they carry on their previous conversation.

Sometimes Niimik visits me on the island. I see his footprints below the porch table, usually after I have eaten fish for dinner. Sometimes I ask one of the kids to thoroughly rinse the fish stringer and hang it up high on the clothesline, where Niimik can't reach it. They rinse it quickly and forget it on the porch table. During the night, Niimik always finds the fish stringer. He likes to lick it like a lollipop, then pull it down through a hole in the boards to the sandy space under the porch. There he snoozes with it, like a security blanket. Sometimes Niimik is a late sleeper, and he stumbles out when I slip out the front door with a cup of coffee to watch for caribou. He always leaves behind the stringer. Most of the time, he leaves an end of it above the boards for me to grab and pull up. Sometimes he doesn't, and I have to fish it out with a stick. "Oh, Niimik," I smile, "can't you find another toy?"

"Why are you sleeping on a nice day like this, Niimik Niigik?" the seagull asked the otter who was sleeping under my porch. "It is so calm, that I can see the minnows down there. Great time to eat."

"Not now," he muttered and rolled over. He moved his tongue around in his mouth. His breath was stale from the fish stringer he'd licked clean on the porch last night.

"I'm not kidding. It's so calm, it's like a mirror out here," chided the seagull. "Hey, look at that beautiful bird with the ring on her beak!" she joked, looking at her own reflection.

Why Are You Sleeping on a Nice Day Like This?

The mergansers harrumphed. They all three simultaneously dipped their faces in the water, as a silent, orchestrated statement to the cheesy wit of the seagull. They raised, threw their heads up, and swallowed. "You are, indeed, a fool for sleeping in, Niimik," one of them announced. "You can see every single crayfish down there. Look and dive. Look and dive. It couldn't get any easier."

A loon glanced over her shoulder, from a bit deeper out in the lake. "You know, Niimik, those cormorants out on the shoal have already feasted. They've got their wings outstretched to dry. They're already resting and digesting. What are you going to do if a stiff wind blows up, Niimik Niigik, scramble for food at the last minute? You really are a slob!"

Niimik Niigik thumped his tail and shifted. He wiped a bit of sand off of his nose and yawned in distaste. The water birds glared as he failed to emerge out from under the porch.

"Sleeper!" screamed the seagull.

"Fool!" muttered the mergansers.

"Slo-o-o-b!" Loon drew out the word to accentuate the insult.

By mid-morning the surface of the lake was moving. By noon there were whitecaps.

By late afternoon, the water birds had fled the open water and had gone for shelter. There they gossiped and felt down-right self-righteous. None of them would venture out in such rough weather. None of them would sit hungry under any human being's porch!

I looked out at the great swelling waves, glad not to be a crayfish, dislodged, thrown recklessly about by the surf. Then I saw that dark spot a few feet from shore. Poor duck, I thought, time to take shelter. But it was Niimik Niigik, the otter, playing in the waves. I could see him chewing up one dislodged, disori-ented crayfish after another—his favorite food! He propelled himself through the steep swells of the waves with his webbed feet and powerful, long tail, smiling, water dancing and happy.

"So glad I saved myself for this. What a feast!" he cooed to himself, as the water birds huddled elsewhere in judgmental ignorance.

It was a quiet morning, and the lake was calm, as Nanaboozhou pulled his canoe up on the rock bank in front of his
blueberry camp. Mink, cheerful and curious as usual,
popped up in his path.

"Hey, so it's you. You must be one rich fella to own
this big, big house!"

"Come inside, Mink. The place is full of mice.
You'll have a feast."

"You come here alone so often. Why would just
one man have such a big, big house? You must be
very rich."

"I come here alone to *be* alone, you chattering
fool. And today someone has to sweep away all
those mouse droppings before the people
begin to arrive. This house is big because I fill
it with all of my relations. They will be coming soon. This is the best blueberry camp in
the whole wide world. The blueberries are
ripe right now, and we need to gather them
for the whole year. It takes many hands to do
the work."

Don't Judge a Book by Its Cover

"There will be many of us here all at once,
many families. This big, big house will feel
small. This house will be full of noisy children
soon. Make yourself useful and catch some of
those mice, before this place gets too noisy even
for you!" Nanaboozhou pointed under the house.

"Where is your smokehouse? Why doesn't a rich
man like you have a big, big smokehouse?"

"Foolish Mink! This is a *blueberry* camp. The lake
is full of walleye. They are good eating for the family
when we are here, but there are other fish that keep
better. We go elsewhere for that. Are you going to eat
some mice or what?"

"You must be a rich man to have such a big, big house just
for blueberries."

"We eat a lot of blueberries. It's not that fancy inside. Come on in. Have a look around. Maybe eat a few mice while you are in there." Nanaboozhou made a sweeping motion with his large hand.

"Wow! This place is a real dump! Why wouldn't you fix up a big, big house like this?"

"It is a temporary home, you idiot Mink! It is only for visiting when the blueberries are ripe. I have a much nicer, smaller house to the south where I keep my garden and where the deer live. The relations have their own houses down there, too. This is how we choose to live. This is the life that our creator gave us. We like blueberries almost as much as you like mice. Go under the house and earn your keep."

It was a quiet morning. Lake Superior was calm, as Nanaboozhou pulled his canoe up on the small patch of dark sand in front of his island house. Goose pulled up a large tuft of grass in front of the doorway and evacuated on the entry step.

"Ennnhhh . . . Thank you, Goose!" said Nanaboozhou, sweeping away the offending goo with a stick.

"Hey, so it's you. You must be one rich fella to own your very own island with all of this nice grass." Goose cocked her head to view him with one eye.

"This is my trout camp. Stop eating my lawn, Goose."

"You come here alone so often. Why would one man have such a big, big island? You must be very rich."

"I come here to *be* alone, you honking fool." Someone has to come here early to sweep away the spider webs. My family will be here soon. Why don't you wander on up to that smokehouse there and eat a few spiders?"

"Why would your family come here? There are no blueberries on this island. You must be a rich man, to keep such a big, big island with no blueberries on it."

"This is a *trout* camp, you nosy Goose. We pick berries elsewhere. Wander on over to that sleep camp down the beach there and eat a few spiders. Mind you, leave the mushrooms alone. They are my favorite."

"Why do you have more than one house on this big, big island with all of this grass? You must be very rich."

"The houses are not fancy. They are temporary homes. We all have nice homes with smaller lawns to the south, where we have our gardens.

"I have a lot of relations coming, Goose. They might get tired of eating pike and trout and decide to vary their diets with a nice, dark *goose;* do you get my drift? You sure talk a lot for one goose. It's a good thing you are so good at keeping the grass cut when I am not here."

It was a quiet morning. The woods were still as Nanaboozhou wound through the old trail to the small wigwam. A Canada Jay perched above the smoke hole, hoping to get a glance at Nanaboozhou's food supply.

"Hey, so it's you. Why would a fellow live in such a tiny, tiny wigwam? You must be very, very poor."

"This is my moose camp, Camp Robber. I'm traveling light. Stay out of my blueberries. Go pick some hazelnuts."

"You come here alone so often."

"I come here to *be* alone. This is my moose camp. It is a solitary activity. It is a *quiet* activity. Stop chattering. Go fill your bill with hazelnuts."

"Why the tiny, tiny wigwam? Are you too poor to share your blueberries?"

"It is my *moose* camp, Camp Robber. I am out in the woods, sitting or moving the whole time. I don't need a big house. I am never in it.

"Now go gather some hazelnuts. You could bury them right there, next to the door of my wigwam. Use a pebble to mark the spot. I'll keep an eye on it for you, heh, heh."

"Why are you too stingy to share?" whined Camp Robber, hopping down even closer, peering into the folds and pockets of Nanaboozhou's buckskin shirt.

"I'm going to haul an entire moose out of the woods. I've got to travel light, foolish bird. I don't have food to share. Why are *you* too stingy to share your nuts?"

"Poor, poor Nanabush, living on just a handful of dried blueberries. Living in such a tiny wigwam."

"I have a bigger, fancier house to the south where I have my garden and where the deer live. I have an even bigger, empty house up where the blueberries grow. I am *not* poor. Here, have a blueberry. Be quiet. Go away!"

It was a quiet morning. The breeze barely tickled the leaves on the dry cornstalks as Nanaboozhou stripped the dead vines away from his pumpkins and squash.

"Hey, so it's you. Nice garden, Nanaboozhou. Good to see you home. When are you going to add an extra room on to that little house of yours?" The neighbor stood with his hands in his pockets.

"Do you want a pumpkin? Pick one out and strip it down yourself."

"I could help you add on to that house of yours. Is your youngest still sleeping in the living room?"

"It's big enough. It meets our needs. There is going to be a frost tonight. I need to get these pumpkins into a shelter. Take one with you if you want."

"All this food to be put away. Why are you out here alone?"

"I come here to *be* alone. You want a pumpkin?"

"Need to get out of that crowded house, eh? You shouldn't be too embarrassed to ask for help, Nanaboozhou. That's what neighbors and friends are for."

"No! No! My house is not too small, Neighbor! I have a big, big house, far to the north, at my blueberry camp. I have *three* other houses, fool! This house is empty! Everyone is staying in a different one today, closing things up for the snowfall. In fact, I'm downright lonesome! Do you want to stick around and help me put away these pumpkins and squash or what?"

"Four houses! You must be very, very rich. I guess you could spare a few of those pumpkins."

"Yup!"

"How about a few of those blueberries, too?"

"Well . . . you know, we go a long way to get them. Just a few."

"Could you spare a few of those smoked trout?"

"I am *not* rich! Did I mention that the big, big house is very simple and poorly furnished . . . just a temporary camp?"

"Got any moose steaks?"

"Did I mention that one of my other houses is just a fish camp?"

"I am not fond of liver. Where do you keep the tenderloin?"

"Did I mention that one of my houses is just a tiny, tiny wigwam?"

Don't Judge a Book by Its Cover

A trout is an aggressive fish. Sometimes I watch trout in the streams and lakes. They have a pecking order among themselves and with other fish. The brook trout is the most aggressive of all, causing considerable jealousy and malfeasance among the fishes.

The fish were known, from time to time, to register a complaint, with Nanaboozhou, their creator. Poor soul, he would merely wander down to the water's edge to relax, to listen to the lapping of the waves, to admire his accomplishments. It always took him by surprise when one of the fishes was dissatisfied. He had tried so hard to make them different, to give them each special gifts, so that every one would fit into its own special niche and feeding pattern.

Fins

"I'm ugly," croaked the bullhead. "I'm bony," griped the lush. "I'm too small to beat the trout to the drowned worms flowing downstream!" squealed the creek chub. "Those brook trout are so vain, with their bright red spots!" hissed the lake trout. "The walleye can see better on the bottom of the lake than we can," complained the whitefish. "My lips are weird," slurped the sucker.

"What is this? Is it the weather, or what?!" Nanaboozhou exclaimed after one particularly difficult morning at the beach. "I gave all of you gifts, but you don't seem to want them. Each of you thinks the other's attributes are better than your own!"

With that, he completely stripped down all of those fish of each of their attributes: color, size, shape, ornamentation, lips, fins, eyes, tails, scales, tongues, jaws, cheeks, and teeth. There they were, equal and naked.

"Now go work it out among yourselves," he shouted, tossing all of the attributes away from himself, out into the open water.

The fish scrambled, fumbled, and reached for one another's special qualities. When they were done, they were pretty jumbled up and unable to cope.

"My top tail fin is bigger than the bottom one," said Sturgeon, morosely. "My eyes are too small. I can't see a thing," complained Walleye, just before swimming into a stump. "Woah! These fins are so big, that I keep propelling myself out of the water!" wailed a minnow, landing on the beach.

"Work it out!" shouted Nanaboozhou, flipping the minnow back into the water.

So, there was a general swirling of water and an occasional splash, as they rearranged themselves, taking back their original body parts. (Except for Sturgeon. No one is sure where that oversized tail fin came from.)

Unfortunately, the brook trout, still aggressive in nature, took one too many fins. This left the lake trout short one back fin. Brook trout wasn't sure what to do with the extra fin in the middle. It didn't help turn to the right or the left. It didn't move the back end or the front end. In fact, it caused the poor creature to swirl helplessly in the shallows. The lake trout was no better off. It simply couldn't turn quickly enough to pursue its prey.

"Stay that way all day. It will teach you two fools a lesson!" laughed Nanaboozhou. He sat in the sunshine to watch them flail.

After a while, Nokomis, Nanaboozhou's grandmother, stopped by to see what her boy was up to. She had heard him laughing and knew that she had better check to make sure he wasn't causing any trouble. Of course, he was.

"Nanaboozhou," she scolded him, "fix those poor fish."

"Just a little while longer, Nokom," he said. "They're making such fools of themselves."

"Don't you remember, Grandson, that you made the brook trout hungry all day long? Without eating all day, the brook trout will grow weak. That aggressive nature is a gift *you* gave that creature. Do you see how it is wearing itself out, trying to continue to eat, with that ridiculous extra fin? And that poor lake trout! Return to it the other back fin, so it can hunt!"

Doing as his grandmother bid, Nanaboozhou whined, "But Grandmother, they were complaining."

"You were vindictive, Nanaboozhou. That is not a gracious way to handle your responsibilities."

Head bent, the spirit followed his grandmother home. Some days, when there are no fish to be caught, and the lakes are hot and still, one can hear her—still scolding him. Her voice is soft, hollow, and incomprehensible, like the bantering of distant waterfowl or the gentlest lapping of the smallest of waves.

The spark plug is misfiring in the boat motor, and the tool to replace it is in the truck back on the mainland. With occasional prodding from a can of flammable WD-40, the boat travels around Lake Superior's cliff-bound Cape Gargantua and glides onto the rocks. We remove the motor, the oars, coolers, quillwork, an empty hundred-pound propane tank, and we carry the boat up 100 feet of unstable boulder beach, hoist and strap it to the bed of the truck, and drive an hour uphill to the paved road, where we almost hit a moose.

Indian Mission Church

While I wait to meet a truck full of boulders that I am to drive down into Michigan's lower peninsula, I do quillwork. I help an uncle mow his lawn. I hold the bottle of transmission fluid and occasionally hand him tools as he works on his truck clutch. Neighbors at a birthday party want to buy quillwork, but I have no completed pieces. Instead I entertain them by making cut and bitten designs with fresh birch bark from the yard. In exchange, a man hands me a book about lighthouses. It is dusty and worn. "It's one of his favorites," a niece informs me. I treasure its dust and the stories we have exchanged.

I drive for hours the next morning, go through customs, then inch the dump truck through the sleepy Sunday streets of Sault Ste. Marie, only to discover that Father John has changed service hours for the summer, and I am three hours early to church. I inch five minutes down the road to Auntie's house, where we are coffeed and fed.

I had eyed a K-Mart on the way into town. I survey the new coffee stain on my hooded sweatshirt. I match my five-year-old. The sleeves are rumpled, rolled up. I have been sweating in my work boots for a week, dismantling a rusted old wood-burning cook stove. There is no space in a boat or a truck for a nice dress or a fancy barrette. I smell like WD-40, wood smoke, and transmission fluid. Father John will understand. He has lived and grown with this odd, tiny congregation of town Indians and occasional Bush Visitors.

At the door Auntie gives the five-year-old the choice of front or back pews. Little Guy adamantly chooses the front, where he knows he can openly protest during the more boring, ritualistic, repetitive portions of the Catholic service. When he opens up the floor to the congregation to make specific prayers to the Lord, the Indian priest will begin by praying that his service not be so boring for Little Guy's sake. Father is a master at his craft. This repartee makes the child love church. Father understands that we sometimes endure a few days of travel to arrive at his church, and that the children can sometimes sit still no longer. He graciously accepts the gift of our presence.

Father John has sung, strummed, and clapped his way to a summer vacation. The Abbot is here instead. A tall, thin, pale man. Handsome, gracious, quiet, and calm. He does not lead us in song with Father John's clear baritone. He leaves us on our own, to hum along with the folks who can read music. The white sash hides his slimness under the white robe. He looks a little more imposing than he actually is. Behind him, the crucifixes are dripping with beadwork. Statues of the Virgin are draped in dance shawls and regalia, and they look ready to step out and twirl among the moose antlers carved into thunderbirds.

As he speaks, we smile attentively into his face, grateful for the sound of another human voice and the moist bodies of the twenty-five or so people in the congregation. After all, that moose was the first thing we had seen that wasn't a caribou. The Abbot came a close second.

I am listening to the story of how Abram had packed up his family and his slaves to go win a battle against the people who had taken his brother as a slave. I cannot help but wonder why Abram, now that the shoe was on the other foot, didn't turn around and set his poor slaves free. I wonder if the first

generations of black robes who "converted" the past generations of my family believed in slavery, because it was taken
for granted in the bible stories. I wonder if this was how they
got all those Indians to build their churches for them in the
old days, or if they did it out of love and faith. If the Indian
priest was around, I wouldn't mind asking. But maybe the
Abbot wouldn't make that automatic association between
slavery and the racial tensions that result in our continued
high unemployment. I momentarily long to be back in the
bush.

Well, maybe it has been longer than a moment. The miles
and hours have taken their toll. The child's ability to sit still has
peaked and is now on a downhill slope. The confined energy
gurgles and bubbles in the front pew like a warm casserole. I
am gently pushing down on a bouncing head when the Abbot
says, "May the spirit be with you." My conscientiousness
strains to participate, and I slip into childhood autopilot. "And
also with you," the congregation murmurs, as I sing out, "Et
avec vôtre es-pii-iir-iiiiiiiiiit . . ." The Abbot's head bolts sideways, and I am found out. Infrequent Visitor. Infidel. French
Singer and Babbler of Thirty-Year-Old Liturgy. Foul-smelling,
two-headed beast in the front row, certain that shame is the
road to Purgatory. I implore with my eyes. Can't you say it all
loud and clear for me like Father John?

The older Indian ladies behind me in the next pew are prim.
When we turn to touch hands and share blessings, I am greeted
with, "He's in your pursssssse." It is a cross between a whisper
and a hiss. I crawl under the pew for a few moments. Better to
lose my wallet than my soul, so I stand up and stare ahead at
the Abbot. I listen to the periodic zipping sound as the ladies
repeatedly retrieve the purse and put it to my shoulder, only to
be yanked from my receiving hand by the short, blatant viola-
tor of the first pew. It is as repetitive as certain parts of the
service. I cannot find my place in the book. Auntie is giggling,
shoving a fingered page under my nostrils. Can't you please
sing it all out loud and clear for us like Father John?

"I am not Father John," the Abbot announces to the congregation, loudly, clearly. "I do not strum the guitar and sing (in Indian) and get you to clap your hands." Perhaps the children need motor feedback to the hypothalamus, I reason, a little wiggling to keep them attentive. I wiggle my wet toes in the rubber boots.

The Abbot is telling us a story about the patron saint of priests. He carefully describes the elegant reliquaried mummy in the French church. He makes the living man himself sound a little bit like the village idiot. He was a simple man, so he was sent to a small, out-of-the-way church, the Abbot explains. Yet he was loved, so loved that people came from miles around to hear him. He likens Father John to this patron saint. I know it is the highest of compliments. Still, doubts creep in, and I find myself wondering if he is not secretly comparing congregations. Never mind the village idiot. We are the idiot village. And I am in the front pew.

A warm breeze has meandered from the open doors in the back. I get a whiff of transmission fluid.

It is time for the offerings. A youth stands patiently with the basket, while I fumble in my purse and hand Little Guy a dollar bill. He refuses to drop it into the extended basket. I shake his hand, repeatedly, hoping it will tumble like a frost-loosened wild hazelnut or a windblown autumn leaf. The child squawks, and I quickly retrieve another bill from my purse, stuffing it wildly into the basket. I look to the Abbot for forgiveness. He hems and haws, smoothes the wrinkles in his robe, trying to buy me a little time in the most gracious way possible. I push down a small, straight, springy arm, waving a dollar bill, as it pops back up, repeatedly, like a young sapling. When his eyes finally meet mine, the Abbot is stifling himself, choking. By grace, I see the fleeting smile, the swallowed laugh. He is a good man, an understanding man, a patient man, and an experienced priest. My soul may be out of danger.

Now the Abbot comes to the part of the service where he asks if anyone has any specific situations for which we might pray to the Lord. At this point, there is inevitably a long, awkward silence. No one wants to be rude by going first. Some of us are caught by surprise and are still thinking of something. I like to ask that I get my kids home safe on the highway. I like to think that I am doing Father John a favor by filling up the void and getting the ball rolling. But the visiting Abbot won't know the details of this trip to church—how the government closed off the road to the sandy harbor, my sweat-drenched boat-dragging clothes, the big diesel truck full of masonry rocks in the parking lot, where a freshly spilled half pint of milk oozes into the warm upholstery of the seat. I am silent.

Inside the tiny church, the group silence is longer than usual. People are shy in front of the Abbot. Then it happens. It comes bold and clear from under the front pew. "MOM, I PEED IN MY PANTS." Behind me the entire congregation of two dozen chants for the first time with uninhibited enthusiasm, "Lord hear our prayer."

I try to imagine the first *married* Ojibwe man to obtain a pair of scissors through trade. Perhaps he obtained the tool in exchange for wild rice or fish from another Indian who had in turn exchanged it from yet another man. The exchange might have taken place far from any fort or trading post. There is no doubt in my mind, however, that the first married Indian to bring home a pair of scissors lost possession, permanently, within five minutes.

Ojibwe women have long had a love affair with scissors. It was passed down to us from our mothers and grandmothers, in a cascade of generations that goes back hundreds of years. "Hand me that *moooozh wagan,* that woooonderful tool," said the Ojibwe woman into whose hands ultimately fell that first pair of scissors obtained in trade. It would have become an indispensable part of her kitchen routine, something her daughters and her daughters' daughters would eventually take for granted, except for the name: Wonderful.

That Wonderful Thing

Moozhiwagan is the word that Ojibwe women have given to scissors. It means, "that wonderful thing." We have chosen to give scissors a place of honor within our language. Wonderful is a big part of our lives. The birth of children is wonderful. A new vaccine is wonderful. A time saving invention is wonderful. And so, scissors are wonderful.

Even as recently as my own childhood, scissors were far stronger and more durable than the scissors of today. No plastic handles to break, these. They were of one piece, both handle and blade. No rivets to pop out. They were held together with screws, easily tightened with a knife blade. They were sharpened on a grinding stone, later on a grinding wheel, and even later by itinerant knife sharpeners. A pair of scissors lasted more than one lifetime and was handed down within the family.

The uses that my mother and grandmothers found for this tool were boundless. A favorite use was for butchering animals. I still use scissors today for that purpose and to cut away fat from store-bought cuts of meat. I use them to cut long, heavy filets of lake trout and pike into human-sized portions. I use them to cut and sculpt heavy sheets of birch bark into strong baskets.

I use scissors to cut papery thin birch bark into delicate, lace-like, folded multiple images of leaping deer and dancing otters. I cut out pictures of grazing bears, swimming turtles, fishermen, basket makers, and all of my ancestors at work and play. I make these images of so many different wonderful things, but I do it with only one tool: *That Wonderful Thing.* That pair of scissors that makes for straight, clean cuts with only one pass and little risk of injury. That wonderful thing that makes for speed and accuracy. That wonderful thing that rivals the snowshoe, the copper fishhook, wild rice, medicines, corn, and all the good things we had that the Europeans borrowed from us. Score one point for the European invaders. They had, indeed, come up with a good one. Still, no one but the Ojibwe had the sense to single out that one tool and give it a name worthy of its stature in the American household: *That Wonderful Thing.*

My mother hung an open pair of scissors on the wall of her kitchen. So did her mother. As children, we were told jokingly that it was to keep away evil spirits. The only evil spirits we could think of were the rust spirits. If we were caught hanging the scissors squeezed shut, we were made to dry them and open them immediately. My mother oiled her scissors, along with her cast-iron pots and pans, to protect them from the damp climate. We had only one pair of scissors for the household. It was put away promptly after each use. To lose the scissors verged on sin. Siblings eyed one another with a vengeful hope of each catching the other in wrongdoing, forgetting to put away the coveted scissors. Scissors were power. Scissors were opportunity. Only the most respectable and dependable of children could be relied upon to use a pair of scissors, let alone safely carry one across the room.

That Wonderful Thing. That source of confusion. That singular pair of scissors made up of two halves, each called a scissor, and neither complete nor especially useful without the other. Put together a scissor and a scissor, and one has a singular pair of scissors. Put together a scissor and a scissor, and one has scissors, plural. In Ojibwe, the tool is but one. There is no confusion. There is only one wonderful thing, *that* wonderful thing. That pair of scissors that lightens one's workload and reduces errors. That wonderful shaper and trimmer of paper and cloth, leather and treebark, flesh, fresh greens, and twine. The word has remained unchanged for centuries, even though the concept of wonderful has faced competition from the sulfur match, modern medicine, the steam engine, electricity, and the computer. There is only one tool that has attached itself so readily and easily to the intents and tasks-at-hand of Ojibwe women for generations. I turn to my daughter, "Hand me the *moozhiwagan.*" She does so reluctantly, eyeing my placement of it when I pause in use, ready to snatch it away, to use it, to store it away carefully, to covet.

When she first started dating Epanigishimoog, her mother was a little bit worried. He professed to be the West Wind, and indeed, he kept unusual hours. He came and went at whim, and seemed to be an unreliable sort. All sorts of rumors about their relationship have circulated over the years, and through the generations, and since Winona is no longer here to defend herself, I can't help but wonder about the sources of the various tales and rumors that abound.

Each contributor to her oral history, it seems, has brought his or her slant to the story over the years. There are those who say that the father of Winona's children was an untrustworthy sort, that he was a typical male, leaving the mother to raise the children alone. This may reflect the personal experiences of the teller, as there are others who say that it was an honor for Winona to have been selected as a wife by someone as powerful as the West Wind. After all, he had an entire continent to tend to, lakes and beaches to sweep, rainstorms to deliver, greedy fishermen to scare off of the lakes, fish spawn and toads' eggs to scatter, as well as milkweed and all sorts of seeds to distribute. He had something of a time schedule to follow, when he could, bringing in the heaviest of storms and gales in the late fall and winter, resting for days at a time during the lazy heat of summer. He took only brief pauses at dawn and dusk . . . when he could, when there were not pressing issues to pursue. . . . He was a busy man . . . a mysterious man . . . what we call a *manido*, a spirit.

The Winona Dilemma

Only a powerful, honorable woman could assume the responsibility of raising the four boys of a spirit being. Half spirit and half human, they were a handful for the woman! All boy, all powerful. . . . Surely she did her best in raising them. Yes, it is all in the outlook of the storyteller.

It is said that Winona and Epanigishimoog had four boys, each raised in a different generation. Again, there are those who say she let this spirit man use her for far too many years. There are those who don't venture to explain the time reference; they simply say that things were different in the old times; that there were giants and that time meant nothing. There are others who think that it means that this loving, caring couple, ancestors to so many of us, lived long enough to see four generations. They became great grandparents. This was not so unusual, back when people married so much younger . . . when was that . . . earlier in this century?

Perspective. Storytellers tell their own stories. They don't mean to. They let their life experiences and ideas slip in between the bits and pieces of history that have come to them. There are so many versions among us, of this first woman, this mother of Manaboozhou, Nanabush, our goofy, loving, mixed up teacher and hero. They are all valid. They are all real. They are all traditional. None of us knows them all by heart. We take the parts that we need and understand. These are the stories that we share with our children. In a sense, that makes us all a little bit like Winona and Epanigishimoog. We are the creators of the *Anishnabe* generations who come after us. I like that responsibility.

Personally, I lean toward the kinder, more understanding version of Winona and the West Wind, but I understand the need for harsher versions as well. Sometimes harshness does not come merely from bitterness. Frightening stories and tales of misadventures or deadly relationships are preventive in nature. They are ways to encourage our children and loved ones to avoid our errors and the mistakes we've observed: cultural shorthand, a form of beseeching others not to learn the hard way. To me, this implies that the West Wind is, indeed, a harsh character—and for good reason. Relationships can be as harsh as weather systems. The West Wind *is* powerful, *is* unreliable, *is* deadly . . . and, well, ya gotta love 'im for it. Nobody else is big enough to do the job, except maybe a storyteller.

The Winona Dilemma

Calm Days

For Uncle Dick

Grandfather has not lived alone in his old home for two years now. In his youth, a road had stretched for miles through the woods to the harbor beach where he launched his boat. The road was closed off by the government, however, when the virgin timber was gone. For decades, he bumped and wound his way around stumps the size of cars, in an old truck and by snow machine, even by snowshoe. He lived without telephone, mail, electricity. He hunted. He fished. He trapped. He lived by his own strength and wits, comfortable in the knowledge that he had raised and provided for his seven children, and that each was now independent and safe. However, the old man can no longer single-handedly heft a small boat over his head and carry it a full ten minutes from the nearest lingering spur of dirt road to the rocky shore of the lake. He has become dependent upon others, upon our schedules of family and work, because he can no longer lift the boat alone.

One End of the Boat

He insists upon lifting the motor himself, as I've watched him do all of my life. I run down the rocks after him, finally able to grab the propeller end from the stubborn old man. "I had no idea it was so easy when someone was helping," he laughs, implying that he could have used my help years sooner. It has always been like that with him, sentences that never needed completion, the smiles, the absolute level of comfort, lack of ego, and endless humor. The old steelworker's muscles still ripple under the weight of the vessel, the motor, and the groceries, even though he is less than steady, as we trek back and forth with a week's worth of supplies.

It is so hard for me to get away, so that he can spend time on this remote island on the north shore of Lake Superior. A little piece of him dies every day that he is not here. I do not fear for his safety here, where there are no other houses for thirty miles in either direction. He is perfectly in control here, and I would not grieve for him if he died alone out here. Rather, I worry for his continued happiness away from this place. I do not come along to babysit him. I only come to hold one end of the boat (and because a little piece of me dies every day that I am not here).

"Gey-goh, Miisho," I urge the old man, "please don't." He is driven by a hunger that originated in childhood, a learned taste, for wild eggs so sweet, that no grocery store product can compete. Wild eggs, fresh and wonderful. Not the flat, runny, sulfury store-bought kind. There is a quality known only to the most refined of palates. Wild eggs are better than chicken eggs fresh out of a chicken. They come from healthy, active birds with a good diet. They hit the palate with a sweet tang not unlike a tree-ripened peach.

As a child, I ate wild duck eggs. I had always lived on the water. Often, in springtime, young inexperienced ducks would, in utter surprise, drop their first clutches of eggs on the beach. Clustered by sex and age, the young females each left a fresh mistake daily, first thing in the morning, when the air was still cool. I used to go out early and scoop them up, before the raccoons ate them, often three in a morning within a span of a few feet. Nature would not leave them lying out on the open sand long enough to spoil. My favorites were the mallards' eggs. Their huge eggs were a light turquoise blue. Finding them was like a holiday. We ate them immediately, fried soft, without anything on them, not even salt.

Gathering seagull eggs is different. Young gulls rarely leave eggs on sandy beaches. They tend to lay their camouflaged eggs in rocky and pebbly areas, preferably on isolated jetties and islands. Their eggs look exactly like World War II army-green camouflage uniforms. The abandoned eggs of the youngsters cannot be separated out from the eggs of the more experienced mothers. Gulls will lay a replacement egg each time a fresh one is taken, and brief human exposure does not keep the gulls from returning to their nest sites in an area where

Fried Eggs

only one house lies within seventy miles of coast. The nests are small, rocky indentations where lichens, mosses, and grasses from the previous growing season are dry and soft like hay. Taking eggs for a few days will not affect the population.

One watches the gulls. When a few birds come in to a new area to nest, three or four nests on the lower edge of the rookery are observed for new eggs. These nests are most vulnerable to otters and other egg-eaters. After two or three days, new nest sites are selected, so that no individual birds are stressed out physically or emotionally. This gathering drama can be carried out for weeks, as new gulls arrive to lay. In the old days, the eggs were water-cooled, then wrapped and buried deep in sandy areas next to people's waterfront homes, where the water table from the big lake kept the eggs cool and edible for weeks. Even now, Grandfather pre-cools the eggs in Superior's frigid spring waters before storing them in an aged, round-cornered, propane-fueled Servel.

Today the old man takes advantage of Lake Superior's mid-Spring calm. He steers the small boat over glassy, sunlit waters, between treacherous shoals that could not possibly be traversed under any other circumstances. Our *agwaa,* our landing place, is bare rock, only inches above the flat surface of the unmoving water. The rock is pocked with bits of aluminum boat scrapings from this man's lifetime of calm spring waters. The tang of sweet, fresh eggs is on the tip of his tongue. It has been two long years.

It is only ten days before solstice, the longest day of the year. I have been trying to tell him it's too late. But he has insisted. My heart breaks at the thought of taking a partially developed egg, a life interrupted. "We'll see," he insists. "You never know. We couldn't get here any sooner." I comfort myself in the probability that warmth and weight distribution will tell us to leave the eggs where they sit.

I set my five-year-old son on the warm rocks, feet down, like a sack of potatoes. "Don't move," I tell him, "Look for the eggs. Watch every step." And the old man, light on his feet like a fairy, dances up the rough surface, pointing out each camou-flaged egg to the awestruck child. The adults scurry up the rock slopes, not too quickly, hoping to lure us away from their off-spring, hopeful that camouflage will keep them safe. Chuck-ling, Mishomis scoops up a chick—large, speckled, the colors of lichen-dotted volcanic rocks. His gentleness and self-assured-ness leave me embarrassed, as I realize that he knew exactly what we'd find, that this gift is as sweet as new eggs them-selves. I freeze in my mind the image of the boy, only five, in an oversized windbreaker, on this warm, windless day, caressing his first gray gull chick, while Lake Superior stands motionless, breathless, holding us in time. This day is not about eggs. This day is about secrets from within the bosom of the great lake. I feel shame that it has taken me five years to teach the boy.

Pushing off the boat from the rocks while keeping one's boot dry is an art form. Manipulating the weight and balance of the boat has become second nature to this family. We glide silently away, taking the time to watch activity return to nor-mal on the islet, before breaking the silence with the tiny two-and-a-half horsepower motor. The gray mottled rocks begin to squirm, as the chicks begin to move again, looking up to their returning parents for food. A few chicks had moved as far as two feet away, when they had thought that our attention was averted. Now those few scooted back, to their burrows of rock and debris.

One curious, large chick followed us out to the water, swim-ming after us for a few feet. We shooed it back to the safety of its parents, laughing, relieved to have caused no problems, for all the vast education on the boy's behalf. It is not about sur-vival anymore, though. The boy will eat store-bought chicken eggs all of his life. It is about the old man's need to share the learning, the skills, the values. This may be one of the last little boys to understand the old ways, the intelligence, the common sense, the freedom of a northern world full of resources for the *Anishnabeg*. Few needs were unmet. This old man is no fool.

The Little People of the North Woods

Epanigishimoog is resting. This monstrous, overwhelming being, the Wind Himself, is sound asleep. This is an opportunity on Lake Superior. This is when the Little People spring forth from the forest floor, fall into their tiny boats, and play and explore where the lake offers itself up to every bit of land touching its otherwise restless borders. Great, hulking cliffs are warm and touchable. Islands and coves known only to the clattering hooves and scratching toenails of caribou, moose, bears, and otters come alive with Superior's people, the *Anishnabeg*.

There are those who believe that the Little People are figments of our imaginations—that the Ojibwe believe in fairies. But we are the Little People ourselves, dwarfed by our environment, by old growth timber, by lakes and rivers that are so immense they seem endless. We are one and the same. Sometimes we are very big, and sometimes we are very small. When Epanigishimoog sleeps and Superior opens her arms to us, we are very small.

The water is so clear today that we hang over the edges of our tiny boat, intrigued. Cliffs rise up straight below us, and we float on the dense water that rises above their peaks. We see fifty feet down, clearly, as though we are eagles in a cloudless sky. Lake trout roll their marble-sized eyes up at us and loll but a few feet to one side or another. There is no constant lapping, sloshing, crashing of waves to hide us from the wildlife, not even a ripple. We will see no swimming bears today. The caribou will not come to visit. Only Little People like us and smaller mammals like beavers and otters skitter about on a day like today. We are as much a part of this lake as the crayfish.

We land our small craft and scramble on rocks that are rarely dry and safe to the tread of an awkward human being.

Our eager hands cradle open geodes and vast cauldrons worn smooth by ice-dropped boulders swirled for years in heaving waves. We walk on coarse lava that is creased and caked like old gravy, frozen since the moment that liquid rock hit cool air. It is only here, at Superior's fingertips, that the centuries of soil and softer rock are cleansed from the surface of the lava. No lichens can survive here to tear at the surface structure of this hardest of rocks. We clamber about, we Little People, small, noninvasive, flitting, elusive, and timeless. We are among the secrets of this lake.

The island is so small that I have never dreamed of landing on it. It is perhaps five acres. It is close to the big island, but surprisingly, separated by a chasm a hundred feet deep. Its rocky shore is somehow different from the adjacent island. It is out on the open water's side of the big island. Epanigishimoog rarely leaves this islet alone. I have never dared venture around it. I assume I am being given a tour of its perimeter. I keep my eyes down and ahead for unknown shoals. But Grandfather guides the boat directly onto the rocks. I shift my weight toward the back, and the high front end barely scrapes. We set the anchor on the shore, although today no gust will move the vessel while we are away.

"I'll go this way. You two go around on the other shore."

"But Miisho, I want to go with *you!*"

"No. Follow your mother. Go on. I've got a surprise for you."

In a few minutes, we meet on a rock bluff at the narrow, inland tip of the island. By late morning, this calm day has become so warm that we have left a trail of clothing layers among the rocks. We kneel to sip water directly from the big lake.

"Ohhh . . ." he says with such disappointment. "I wanted to show you a caribou." I am quizzical. I have seen a hundred caribou. Why would a caribou hunker down on this tiny islet with so little forage?

"I figured if I walked around this way, I would make it come right out at you."

I've had caribou run right past me. It's terrifying. So I smile and shrug. I look to the bigger island, where I know the caribou bed down, perhaps 200 feet away from here. I peer into the cedars. Are they watching us? Are they laughing at us?

I return to my knees, for another drink, wondering what sort of sight I am to those caribou, a rare mammal drinking at the water's edge on a calm, hot day. As I swallow, I catch a flicker of movement out of the corner of my eye, before I hear the deafening clatter of those immense hooves. Confused by our prattle, then startled by the actual sight of us, the great beast pulls its weight forward and dashes with unruly momentum into the water. His chest and chin are clearly reflected in the water's mirror-like surface before him. As he propels himself, I see each leg under the surface in its strong paddling motion. It is the biggest caribou I have ever seen in my life.

"One of the cows calves in there." Mishomis points to an old Indian copper mine, a man-made depression in the rock, now full of small trees and lichens. "He just comes to visit." He is referring to the caribou as if it is an old friend. I can imagine them, the two old bulls, in quiet conversation.

The old man is laughing with his whole body. He loves being right. His arms dangle down, and he is helpless, giddy. Today is about teaching. It is about knowing everything about one's environment that one needs to know to survive. The Little People can never have hoped to hunt and live off of animals as immense as bears, caribou, and moose without knowing everything there is to know about them.

Mishomis is not showing off. He is teaching lessons about the *Anishnabeg* that are bigger than hunting. We no longer rely strictly upon hunting for our food. He is teaching me about self-respect and the knowledge that Indians always have been cunning. Our environment and our resources have changed. But we are still smart and adaptable. We are still strong. We know this about ourselves, even if it is one of the best kept unintentional secrets in North America. The Little People should never remain small. We should always know how and when to make ourselves big. As the old man convulses with laughter in

The Little People of the North Woods

front of the fading wake of the great swimming caribou, he stands there as a giant.

And now it is time to become small again, to slip off of the tiny island without further disturbing mother and calf.

Today is a day of transformations. It is a day to feel good about ourselves. It is a day to smile at the silliness of strangers who believe that we are superstitious, ignorant fools who are mistaken in our beliefs that we have actually seen our elders transform themselves into creatures and fish. Today has been a day for flying over mountaintops, while trout, pike, and sturgeon sail through canyons below.

I am not surprised that the fancy dance shirt that would fit a twelve-year-old boy would end up on the downwind shore of Lake Superior, on the side of the big island that faces the open water. I am not even surprised that it still has a ballpoint pen from a casino in its pocket, nor that the pen still works.

But I am absolutely dumbfounded that the shirt found its way into this narrow, convoluted rock-enclosed bay. It is a mystery of currents, a study in the movement and churning of water along straight-sided underwater cliffs and over boat-breaking shoals. It is a miraculous gift from the lake.

The Storeroom

That is why I leave it here. It is not my place to take it. It is neither a curiosity, nor a tourist item. It is lovingly adolescent, overdone, with a bit too much of everything. It is a boy's dream shirt, the ultimate dance shirt. There is a large silk-screened bear on the front, and ribbons sewed in rows. Miles of ribbons. Enough ribbons to make even a twelve-year-old happy. It wasn't lost on a beach on a camping trip. It is his intentional gift to the lake. It is his way of thanking the lake for its gifts of food and nourishment and its endless days of entertainment, trials, and teaching. It is a step toward transition from boyhood into the mysteries and responsibilities of young adulthood. The shirt pulses with power. Once bright and new, it is now torn and faded by the great lake, but still impressive and intact, a leaf-litter-bearing bundle of cotton and polyester.

That is why I leave it here. I leave it here for Manaboozhou's wife. I know that she strolls this protected stretch of small, rock-strewn beach. I know that she climbs the steep thickets here, one hand over another, grasping at the fragrant Labrador tea. I know that she picks her way through the shrubs and dried twigs to a spot at the top where snowberries ripen. She and I are the only ones who know about the snowberries. They are big, white, and deadly-looking. They compress on the tongue like ripe strawberries, only sweeter, and with a mild fragrance of wintergreen. This patch yields only two small handfuls each year—one for her, and one for me. Getting to them is no small chore. We each leave a little for the other.

That is why I leave the shirt here for her. A gift from a twelve-year-old boy, thrown up to her by a huge lake that measures its centuries in tens. . . . Out of respect, I leave it for her, like the berries. She will know what to do with it, as she has done with all the others, in centuries she measures in tens. . . .

Minwaudeniimikwe is an amazing woman, a woman of patience. A good part of her strength is derived from her trying marriage to Manaboozhou, half human and half spirit. He is a fool, a teacher, a trickster, self-centered, and prone to temper tantrums. It is he who has helped the Great Spirit form and shape our world, often through trial and error. He is our greatest teacher, simultaneously regarded with respect and humor. I know that the boy left the shirt for him. But it is his wife who knows what to do with it.

She washes the brittle cedar debris out of the shirt. She stands knee deep in the cold lake, rinsing sand from the fibers, dunking the heavy shirt over and over, occasionally stepping back on to the beach to warm her toes. She walks down the open beach to a place where dark, flat rocks absorb the sun. She pins a corner of the shirt with a toe and twists the remaining water out of the fabric with both hands. The shirt is laid smooth, to catch the remaining light of the day.

Minwaudeniimikwe folds the soft, faded shirt. She has carefully repaired every tear caused by water pounding the fabric against the rocks.

"Manaboozhou, what do you want me to do with this shirt?"

"Will it fit me?"

"Of course not. Don't be silly. It's a child's shirt."

"Let me look at it. Heh, heh. Child's shirt all right. Those boys really like bears don't they?"

"They think that Bear will make them strong."

"That's why it's a boy's shirt. Eventually he'll learn that even a rabbit or a frog can teach him as much. Children think big. They want to learn everything all at once, without the trouble of a whole lifetime of mistakes."

"That's why the *Anishnabeg* love you so much, Manaboozhou. We don't have to learn from our own mistakes. We have you to do it for us."

If looks could kill. . . . But their chuckling is soft as pine boughs, and the two great spirits lean their heads together briefly to share a whispering kiss.

"What do you want me to do with this shirt?" asks Minwaudeniimikwe, brushing a chickadee from her long hair. "It's beat up, looks like it washed up all the way from Minnesota."

"Put it with the others."

"You are going to have to build me a new *dassowigwam, Nimanakewiss,*" she chides, in her leisurely pace toward the largest outbuilding.

"If I were such a bad boy, would I be going out to tend the nets?" asks the spirit, staring out over the calm waters. He dips his great head as a hawk darts by and, with one toe, pushes his great canoe out into the still lake.

Humming softly to herself, Minwaudeniimikwe stands in the doorway of the huge bark storage building, as her eyes adjust to the dim light. Her husband, in his zeal, has greatly overbuilt the structure. It was meant to last, and indeed it has, for hundreds of generations. Its framework is of great cedars—tall but still solid and not yet hollow. Its uprights are bigger around than a man, and the horizontals are half that girth. The woman can barely see to the ceiling. The entire exterior of the building is layered with great sheaths of cedar bark, each overlapping and tied in place with bark and roots. Along the left wall, floor to ceiling, are shelves built of cedar twigs notched and twined carefully into place against the solid framework of the building itself. Manaboozhou built several strong ladders into the framing itself, so that his wife would not have to move a ladder from place to place along the immense wall.

Grabbing with her toes and pulling with her hands, she climbs up several times her own height. The boy's shirt is resting on her shoulder. "I'll put it with his grandfathers,'" she says to herself, patting the worn fabric. One last time she smoothes the wrinkles from the mended and folded shirt, then sets it atop a great stack of soft, yellow shirts of tightly woven cedar bark and porcupine fir. She smiles as her knuckles brush the soft, ancient fabric. They don't make cloth like this anymore.

On this downwind end of Lake Superior, the currents between the islands do unusual things. They churn in great cyclones whenever the wind shifts direction, from northwest to southwest and back again. This scouring, caused by the wrap-around effect of waves unbroken by the full length of the great lake, leaves great underwater sandbars with sheer cliffs. It causes sand beaches to deposit on the shore in unlikely places, far from the nearest river or stream.

My Favorite Fish

Directly across from Mishomis's tiny island home, over on the nearby mainland, is one such beach. The strong wrap-around currents hit an underwater obstacle, then dump their load and speed up again, cutting a deep channel. This creates an odd combination of shallow and deep, of slow-moving and fast-moving water right next to one another. That is why the caribou use one small, rocky patch of shore, and not the nearby beach, to swim to and from the mainland. Their traffic is quite predictable, given the wind direction on any particular day.

Today, when the water is like glass, we scour the mainland drop-offs. Early in summer, the water is free of algae bloom, and visibility is at its greatest in these channels around the coastal islands. "The *Barneys* will be sunning themselves in the shallows today," Grandfather has insisted. He refers to the sturgeon as Barneys. For half an hour we inch along and dangle our fingers into the water over the green sandbars singing, "Heeeere, Barney." We have no luck and return home for lunch.

The search has inspired familiar sturgeon stories. They are good stories. I can listen to them over and over. But, since the old man is talking with his mouth full, we stare out the window past the dock, where mergansers are paddling by, staring down for food, arching and dipping at each morsel, chewing with their mouths open. . . .

Sturgeon are amazing fish, and I never get to see them often enough. They can live for hours out of the water. That is why, in the old days, Indian fishermen were cautious if a sturgeon was the first fish they caught. They always tried to catch something else instead, so that they could slip the sturgeon back into the water as soon as possible. Sometimes this was difficult. A large sturgeon could fill up a small boat or canoe and practically had to be straddled by a contientious fisherman. Sturgeon taste wonderful, and their springy, cartilaginous backbones make wonderful glue, but they reproduce slowly, and the *Anishnabeg* have always known to harvest them sparingly, or as a last resort.

And there's more to it than that. . . . Sturgeons have wonderful personalities, like dolphins. They are curious and love people. To take advantage of that part of their nature would be like abusing a child or a pet. According to tradition, to overharvest sturgeon would be amoral. A sturgeon that allows itself to be caught does so as a great gift.

One day, a small boat with two young Indian fishermen showed up at this very dock. In rough weather, they had inadvertently set their nets too shallow and had caught a sturgeon. It was alive, but appeared to be under stress. They did not know if the animal would live and hated to waste a resource by simply throwing it back into the lake. It was not their target species, and they would not keep it.

So they decided to give it to Uncle Bill, an Irishman married to an Indian. They had assumed that he would have no qualms about eating the fish if it did not survive.

The boys pulled the boat up to the part of the beach that was sheltered by the huge timber dock. Uncle Bill brought the wheelbarrow to the water's edge. They clambered out into knee-deep water, still wearing their pants and shoes. The sturgeon was four feet long, and it took both young men to carefully heft it out of the boat, while Bill steadied the wheelbarrow.

Bill wheeled the fish into the shade and began pouring buckets of water over it, making sure that its gills stayed submerged and being careful to wet all of its skin, so that it would stay comfortable. Every few minutes, Bill would dump fresh buckets of cool water over the sturgeon, trying to insure it a steady oxygen supply. The fish never flopped or moved, but followed Uncle Bill's every movement with its eyes.

Bill eventually found this disconcerting and resolved himself to return the beast to the lake. This sturgeon was, after all, quite young and stood a good chance of recovery. Bill contemplated the supplies he had on hand and dismissed the idea of quickly constructing an impoundment to contain the fish, since the lake was not particularly still that morning. Even small lapping waves move heavy things back and forth near the shore. That is why the huge dock was constructed of timbers and tons of large rocks.

At this point in the story, Mishomis, the man who single-handedly rebuilt this particular dock after a severe storm, swallows and giggles. "Do we have any Clamato juice?"

And so the story is interrupted by general rummaging through the cupboards under the kitchen bench. While the old man was not looking, I had organized the canned goods by category. I had tried to put the oldest-looking cans in front, so that they could be used first, before they rusted through, leaked, and left the shelves sticky and poisonous. After wiping the grit and sand from a rusty can and checking it for leaks where bacteria might have entered, we find Grandfather's favorite glass and get him settled in again. We already know the story, but we want more details. We do not like Clamato juice, but watching him drink it is the price we have to pay.

The next part of the story amuses Grandfather a great deal, and it is hard to get him to stop laughing and continue. We don't care if he talks with his mouth full, we want details.

Uncle Bill decided to tie a rope snugly around the girth of the sturgeon, between its fins, and tie it to the dock. This worked, and the fish seemed more comfortable.

My Favorite Fish

I look out the other window toward the open door of the boathouse, where I know several ropes are coiled up, hanging on pegs along a sidewall. What kind of rope did he use? Is it still there? Have any of us used that same sturgeon-holding rope? In our family, that piece of rope has become famous.

Now, Uncle Bill's wife had grown up hearing *Anishnabe* stories about sturgeon who liked their bellies and sides rubbed and who spoke with human beings regularly. So Alice waded out in her bathing suit to comfort the fish. At first the young sturgeon was quite surprised, but soon it began turning this way and that, in response to Alice's rubbing and petting, and it eventually began to hum softly and sing to itself.

Like a hedonistic house cat, the sturgeon was insatiable. Periodically, Aunt Alice would have to come to shore to rest and relax and to warm up her toes. But the fish stared at her so woefully and longingly, that she kept wading back in to pet its smooth, silvery flanks. Each time, the sturgeon sang more loudly than before. Each time Alice withdrew to the shore, the fish raised such a fuss, that the whole family began to take turns cooing and cuddling it. This was more than Uncle Bill could bear, and after a few hours, he untied the rope and shooed the animal out past the drop-off at the end of the dock. It disappeared into sixty feet of water. By this time, Bill and Alice had named the sturgeon Barney.

Within the hour, Barney was back. Eventually, he was weaned to a few minutes of cuddling a day. After a week, Uncle Bill returned to his job at the steel mill, and Aunt Alice and the children accompanied him.

"I tried to go out and pet him a little bit whenever I saw him there," said the old man. "But, you know, I was busy . . . and it was Alice he really liked."

We have asked him a hundred times if the sturgeon ever comes back, but Mishomis is evasive. He smiles and assures us, "Maybe we'll go out and look again later, if the sun is still in the shallows."

I look. Every time I am knee deep in that lake rinsing laundry, I look. I stare past the drop-off, where it is so deep I can't see a thing. "Barney . . ." I whisper. "Barney. . . ." When they boat across to the mainland, to the big, sandy beach there, I hear my children's voices carry clearly across the calm water, "Baaarneeey. . . ."

W e've often gone to Mishomis's island home without him, to rest and play, to work and recover. The door has always been open, and we have come to regard it as much a part of our lives as our own childhoods.

Past the *waukegon*, the log cabin we call the "sleep camp," the shore gets rocky and cliffy. There in the nooks and crannies of rough shore, Superior throws up well-seasoned wood, great trees. Some are birch smoothly beaver-hewn, and others are large hollow cedars that died standing up and were eventually pulled into the lake by crashing waves.

One year Superior threw a fine drum onto a high and dry rock shelf, just for us. It was a piece of hollow cedar, about five feet long and perhaps three feet wide. The outside wood

The Drum

was firm and smooth, but very thin. With a solid beaver twig as a drumstick, it had a high, warm pitch which could be manipulated by the location on the log the "drum" was struck. For several summers, we sat on the warm rocks, with our backs to the cliff, and sang every Indian song we knew.

There is another island, directly across from that place. Sometimes we hit smooth stones onto its shore with a baseball bat, it is so close. In that rocky hollow where the drum washed up, the sounds bounce back and forth between the two harsh shorelines. The adjacent island gets so loud that we call it "the Fawcett." When the waves are causing a great ruckus on the Fawcett, we are prone to sing a little louder, to get a little sillier. We have been known to sing the Ojibwe version of "Eensy Weensy Spider," followed by a screeching version of "Skinnamarink-a-do," all the more hilarious in Ojibwe. It is a good time. I feel like a little kid. There is no one there to impress, and to the other wildlife, it is no different than the screeching of gulls.

"I found a perfect piece of wood down the beach for my fire tonight," Miisho says. The old man rarely sleeps anymore. He is fond of beach fires and builds big ones where he sits out all night, reliving the years full of days and starry nights. I follow him down the beach, accompanied by a chattering preschooler. We've burned the easy stuff, so now we're hauling home all sorts of immense, rotten, and twisted tree stumps. They are gangly and hard to maneuver, but the old man loves his fires so.

My heart sinks when he stops at the drum, and when my grandfather bends at the knees to lift his end of the log, I obediently dip down and grab my end. We carry it back to the *waukegon,* and I imagine the fun that he will have burning this big hollow thing. But first, I tell him that I've known this log for years, that I call it Little Boy Drum, and the child and I sing for him. We sing every Ojibwe song we know. My son dips at the knees, sways, and sings, all the while beating the drum with a brittle stick that keeps breaking.

The old man finds a good, stiff beaver stick for the boy, and we all sing a strong goodbye to the cedar drum.

"You could burn it upright," I say. "That would really be pretty, with sparks coming out the top."

We sing and drum louder, harder, faster.

"It will be a great log for burning," I say.

I drum harder.

"It's just a log."

Two days go by before I walk down past the ash pile. The drum is still there. I roll it up onto the grass, out of the reach of the waves, next to the caribou path. I don't want to push it too far away from his fire spot. I've let go. I want him to know that he can burn it. I never wanted to deny him the joy of burning it. Boy, am I glad he didn't burn it.

It will never echo as nicely from here, but it still sounds pretty good, in a different way.

The Drum

The storm is over. We are back on the lake again. The trees are full of plastic square milk cartons. They are every color, all along the shore of the mainland and the sides of the islands that face the brunt of Lake Superior's fury. The cartons are printed with the battered and partially legible label of a dairy in northern Michigan, hundreds of kilometers to the west. Perhaps they were blown from a dock or a ship. Maybe somebody else had already found them after a different storm and was already using them on their boat. But to us, they are a gift—a rare, stackable, sturdy, carry-anywhere, waterproof grocery container. So we scour the coastline as though it were Christmas, clambering after the ones that we can safely reach, leaving those that are near dangerous rocks and shoals. The rem- **Superior's Gifts** nant milk cartons will be gone by next year. The lake will tear them from the shoreline trees and deposit them elsewhere.

This year, Superior gave us milk cartons. One year, it was fifty-five-gallon drums of gasoline. Sometimes it gives us notched and squared timbers. We get a lot of little plastic baskets that I think come from a dishwasher. None of us has ever had a dishwasher, but we think we've seen the baskets in a grocery store.

Hundreds of deflated balloons wash up, usu- ally with plastic curling ribbon attached. For every kilometer of downwind coast along Lake Su- perior's shoreline, I would estimate that there is at least one-tenth of a kilometer of plastic curling rib- bon tangled up along the beaches. The ribbons live for years in great plastic snarls among the driftwood and laurels, often with their scissor-induced curls intact. They are death traps to beach-loving flocks of horned larks each fall. In the water, loose ribbons are swallowed up by pike and loons. . . .

Once, when I was alone on the island during a windstorm, a big, blue helium balloon floated past the house on a wild current. It was eerie, more frightening than a bear on the doorstep, because it simply didn't belong in that place. It especially had no business bobbing by as though it had a life of its own. I ran inside and watched it from the window with binoculars, until it disappeared behind another island. I felt compelled to hide, as though it could somehow see me.

It was October. I hadn't seen anybody in weeks. Although I had occasionally heard Virgil's diesel fishing tug go by on the far side of the islands, I was never able to scramble over the half mile or so of rough terrain to where I could catch a glimpse of him, to feel a sense of human contact. I was alone, with a big, blue balloon that looked fresh enough to have been released yesterday . . . a piece of uncaring humankind that had the potential to destroy everything in this place, without ever having seen how harsh and beautiful it is all on its own . . . without plastic snarls.

It's odd how one can find joy in a milk carton and terror in a balloon. A good storm on Lake Superior can play tricks on the mind. It always brings gifts.

My favorite gift from Lake Superior was a Cinderella slipper. We found it out on one of the outer islands, on the bare rock shoals that Superior scours clean. It was pink. Pink with silver sparkles. It had come all the way from Wisconsin during the past winter, we are certain. It had survived months of harsh weather before the lake tossed it up to one small, curious child.

Outside of a handful of wise Ojibwe elders and close family members, few people know the real truth about Cinderella: she is from Wisconsin. And they never found her other slipper when the prince eventually slipped the one in his possession on her peasant foot. She'd lost it in a storm while playing on the beach. Only we know the truth. It's nailed up on our boathouse wall, next to some moose antlers.

"**T**here. There's where I got the log for the boathouse ramp."

It's hard to imagine the handsaw that went through it. Yet I've seen it on his workshop wall. It is buried with the other tools, ropes, nets, and rain parkas hanging over it on wooden wall pegs. It would take half a day to get to it. But now, he uses it only in his memory. It is not at the ready.

The handles on each end of the saw are almost three feet long. It really is a two-man saw, but he always managed to use it himself. The wooden handles are as far apart as the headlights on my car. I can't imagine even carrying it, let alone balancing it in a boat. But the old man was a logger in his twenties. He talks about these mountains and valleys like the rest of us describe our flowerbeds. He knows every logging trail that has grown over, every footpath, every pond, every moose yard. . . .

The Log

"We used to partially block up the streams, to force a temporary little pond, because if we didn't get those logs under water right away, the sawyers would get to them. Sometimes the logs sat for a long time before the teams could get in to pull them out. They had to use horses. It was too rough for trucks. We always broke up the dams when we were done. You can hardly tell we were there. It was a different kind of logging."

We are on the far side of our island, as far from the house as we can possibly get. The cedar stump is immense and hollow. Sometimes we stand inside it . . . all of us, at once. The stump is *immense*. . . .

"Did I ever tell you how I got it back to the house?" he asks.

Of course I know, but I feign ignorance, so he can tell me one more time.

"Did you bring it back by boat?" I ask.

And now he is visibly delighted. By boat is the obvious part, the easy part. Any fool can single-handedly tow an immense tree back to the house on Lake Superior with a chain and a boat. Any fool. The *hard* part is getting it to the water. He is giddy.

Now anybody else might have said that he just left it there, and Manaboozhou did it for him after he went home to rest. But not my grandfather. He doesn't want to share any of the credit. He wants to make sure that I understand all the physics of it, every blessed detail, in case I, a middle-aged housewife, get a hankering to single-handedly cut down and haul a log the size of a Volkswagen back to my house. . . .

"Well, you know how that cedar bark is slippery when it's wet?"

Yes, I know. Whenever big trees were cut, when I was little, we used wide sheets of their bark like sleds, slime side down, and slid down the rocks into the lake. We used to do it when the men built ramadas for pow wows and family picnics. They used to give us the leftover sheets of bark that were too short to fit across the roofing beams. The bark sleds always dried out after a few days, but could be rejuvenated a few times by soaking them in the lake.

"I just peeled off big sheets of it, rolled it onto it, hooked on the chain, and pulled it with the boat."

This, of course, I knew he did after hours of cutting branches and hauling away the brush. In reality, there is no easy part to the whole procedure. It is plain hard work.

We walk back around the island to the house. In some places, we can walk along the rocky shore. In other spots, cliffs force us to climb up into the brush and swing around gnarled, rock-grabbing trees. At one point, we are forced to go through a trail in the woods. Mishomis made it, but the caribou keep it worn down and clear.

The log under the boathouse ramp comes up to my chest, but I think a foot of it is buried in the sand, below my feet. It lies on its side, imposing, sturdy, and hollow. Because it is cedar, it will last most of my lifetime, perhaps even longer, if no freakish pile of late spring ice wrenches it away. But it won't last as many years as a log that lies under water. Which is precisely why I have to pay attention every time he tells the story of how he got the log. I doubt that I'll ever have to do it myself, but I might have to tell the next generation how to do it, after Mishomis is gone, or after I am gone. . . .

I try to imagine his winters here. I try to compare them to my own decades of winters on the mainland. One of our uncles could be visited only when the water was open, or when it was frozen hard, because his home was on a peninsula on a large inland lake, and there was no road to his house. During early winter and late spring, travel was a death trap. The same is true of odd, warmer-than-usual winters. A lot of *Anishnabeg* still live this way. The road to their houses ends at a body of water.

Miisho, however, didn't even have a road nearby, and he never expected the government to maintain a road for one Indian, or to provide postal service for that matter. As long as Lake Superior's water stayed open and storm-free,

Biboon there was always the possibility that he could pick up a quick shortwave radio conversation with a fishing tug. Sometimes, when the cold lake became especially deadly on short notice, Virgil might venture into the convoluted sandbars to tie up the tug to Mishomis's massive dock. Virgil's dad had rebuilt the dock before Miisho rebuilt it. There is an understanding that the dock doesn't really belong to one Indian in particular. Like everything else about Mishomis's ancient island home, it took generations of building and maintenance to take on its current form.

When one comes to know and love the lake, one also comes to fear it. We always urge the youngest of the fishermen to take refuge here when they need it, because we know the young ones are most likely to make an error in judgment. We don't want to read about the recovery of their bodies. In fall and winter, however, those youngsters are just memories. Distant radio reception is unpredictable and scratchy at best, due to the mountainous terrain and the turbulent atmospheric moisture of the Great Lakes. Even listening to radio by battery during clear weather is carefully meted out to oneself. Once the lake freezes up, and the boat is pulled out of the water, there is no way to charge the battery except by generator. And the gasoline that fuels the generator is precious. Propane is precious. Even candles are precious. Matches are stockpiled and kept in waterproof, mouse-proof containers.

Sawblades, axes, and extra wooden handles are oiled and stored carefully. Extra stovepipe and bolts for the mammoth cast-iron, wood-burning cook stove are brought in by boat. Food is selected carefully and stored in moisture-proof containers. Food is chosen for its shelf life, its portability and compact qualities, its ability to nourish the body or soul in adverse conditions.

Seasoned and dried firewood is stored in massive, lidded wood boxes. In summer, they are our tables. In winter, their hinged lids are thrown back against the cabin walls for months on end. Tinder is pressed compactly into buckets in the boat-house. Every scrap of paper is saved all year long, for lighting fires in winter. Every label is saved off of every can of condensed milk. Each empty macaroni box is shredded by hand and ready to use, in case someone gets wet or too chilled and needs a fire instantly. For the same purpose, a great pile of birch bark is made and stored under a protective layer of spruce bows, stacked neatly against the downwind side of the outside woodpile, where it can be dug out from under the snow when needed.

The firewood is divided into two categories, and one needs a constant supply of both. Birch and maple, when maple is available, are the only hard woods here. They are necessary for overnight coals, or to keep the house warm when one is away for hours on end. Cedar catches fire easily and burns quick and hot. It is necessary for starting a fast fire if one is wet or chilled. Hypothermia is the greatest of threats to people living in remote bush camps. The only way to survive is to prepare.

The best firewood comes from living trees, carefully culled from the forest. Dead wood is used only during the warm seasons, and only if it is dense enough. Firewood needs to cure out of doors for at least a season. Grandfather has to store most of his drying wood hidden back inside the bushes and trees. Otherwise, summer visitors from the nearby public campsites steal a great deal of the cut wood for their campfires.

The strangers arrive mostly by canoe. Somehow they feel justified in helping themselves to our supplies, I suspect, because they are so tired from paddling. Or perhaps they feel so alone out here that they cannot imagine that there are a hundred of them, at one time or another, doing the same thing. They feel so small and vulnerable here and are certain, given the splendor of the setting, that the island's owners are wealthy . . . or that the wood, the dock, the propane, even toilet paper, come to this island's residents without extreme effort. In today's world, it is hard to imagine something built over generations, hard labor handed over from one person to another, as an act of love. It is also hard to imagine planning for a long-term stay in a setting this remote, in a house this small.

"Once the lake freezes over between the islands, I catch lake trout through the ice, right there off the dock." As he looks out the window, he is reliving every fish caught.

He canned the extra trout, in pint jars. There are some there still. I open one once in a while, in the heat of summer when no pike, lush, or minnow will bite. He used a 1930 model cast aluminum pressure canner on top of the woodstove. I have the same 1930 model canner. When I order new rubber parts for mine, I order extra for his, too. My mother taught me to can with that big canner, on a cast-iron, wood-burning cook stove. The stove was massive, like this one. I had to watch the pressure gauge and slide the heavy pot around, back and forth between the hottest and coolest spots on the stove's flat surface, depending upon whether or not the gauge dipped or veered precariously high. It's still the best way to can, I think, better than on an electric stove.

Water has always been Mishomis's biggest challenge in winter. When the ice is thin and treacherous, melted snow and ice suffice. It takes a lot of snow to make a pot of cold water. When the ice is safe out front, he can pull it out of holes he keeps open for that purpose. At other times, he throws a bucket on a rope off the end of the dock, if the dock is not glazed over with slick ice, or if waves are not crashing and churning sand into the water.

Our name for winter is Biboon. He has a job to do. He lays his blanket of cold and snow over our mother earth so that she can rest. The snow insulates and protects the plants. Mishomis knows Biboon well. The two old men have spent hours at this same red, wooden table, pushing the pressure canner back and forth, and comparing notes on survival skills.

At times, when Biboon arrives to the house wetter and colder than usual, the old man lends him his old red and black flannel shirt. He makes him a hot cup of tea, or he dips into the ever-boiling stockpot.

"Boozhoo, boozhooooooo Victor!" Biboon howls at the door, until the old man responds.

"Pindegiin," he motions him in. "Aaaambey, you're letting the cold in!" Mishomis shuts the door behind his old friend. "I was just out for half the day. I know just how cold and wet you must feel!" the old man laughs. The snowshoes were tapped clean and left against the outside of the building to stay cold. (Snow would ball up on a warm snowshoe, Biboon taught Mishomis decades earlier.) They silently grunt and huff, untying their boots, hefting them to the shelf on the back wall above the woodstove, where they will dry out.

A chunk of birch is retrieved from the wood box and shoved into the firebox of the stove. For a moment, as the firebox door is opened, thin silver birch smoke escapes through the cracks between the stove parts, as the stovepipe's draw is interrupted. It smells smooth, like the taste of old whiskey.

The two old men rub their cold toes and prop up their feet. They stretch out the kinks from their stiff bodies and laugh about the weather.

"Well, let's see what we've got to eat!" Miisho begins rummaging. "Here is some spaghetti sauce almost thawed. My son made it. He hit a deer down south last winter." He shakes the freezer bag to see if its contents will come out yet.

Biboon pours some hot water from the big kettle into a smaller cooking pot. He refills the hot water kettle to the brim so there will be a steady supply. He grabs the iron lifter and pulls a round burner lid from the hottest side of his host's stove, then slides the pot of hot water over the licking circle of flames. Miisho hands the other old man a box of spaghetti. Biboon's arthritic hands tremble as he pries open the cardboard and breaks the pasta into the now boiling water. He stretches his hands open over the flat iron surface of the stove, to absorb the rising heat.

The old men pass back and forth the salt and pepper, along with a moisture-caked can of Parmesan cheese that they tap over the steaming plates. The food is good. The conversation is good. A can of the coveted Clamato juice is opened up and mixed half and half with beer.

The dishes are washed and the table wiped clean. Now the maps come down from the bookshelf.

The two gray heads bend over the table, for hours. They know every inch of these endless miles of mountains and water, the two of them. They plan, they plot. They decide how the snow and the wind will bend each growing branch, alter each spit of sand, steer each population of bird and mammal. . . .

When the government outlawed snow machines on the adjacent public land, he had to move out. It is not cost-effective for the government to plow the road for one old Indian. Biboon has grown lonesome, and Mishomis longs to be here, to comfort his old friend.

Fear creeps over me when Fog appears when we are out in a boat. She comes from nowhere. She has no origins, no warnings, no rulebook, no mercy. . . . Fog rises up out of the water on the calmest, clearest, hottest, driest of days. Fog pours from the valleys, skitters across the surface of the lake, grabs, envelops, cools, and absorbs every landform and every living thing.

Her name is Kiishigokwe. She is the most benign and loving of spirits. She brings life-giving moisture to the most isolated and desperate of clinging plants and life forms. She recirculates and re-shapes water and wind into much needed pre-cipitation. We call her "the giver of life," and we revere her. We are told to emulate her. And so, like Kiishigokwe, we *Anishnabe* women are the Keepers of the Water. We respect water in all of its forms. We teach our children to care for it and keep it clean. We haul it for our house-hold chores. It seems that women's hands are always in water. . . .

Fog Paints the Landscape

But Kiishigokwe is as human as you or I. She tires, she grows distracted by her children. She lives with her hormones and gets fickle. I have seen her out on that lake, tossing her gar-ments about her head and the treetops. She throws off the mantle of her daily routine and dances like a madwoman about the lake. Her chil-dren run for cover, and her lovers find something else to do, far away from her, or burrowed in a workshop. Even old men cower when Kiishigokwe is angry or wild, or just plain out for a little too much fun. So the *Anishnabeg* run from the lake or crowd Su-perior's shorelines when the Fog Woman is out of sorts or irresponsible.

I save little bundles of tobacco for these events of hers, tucked into the bottom of a deep jacket pocket, below the hard candy and the used tissues, next to the lint. Small bundles of to-bacco that have been gifted to me by others. *Seymuh* is not to be hoarded. It is to be used in thanks and prayers, and occasion-ally in beseeching. People who have given me tobacco have en-trusted me to do the right thing with it. Today I am doing the right thing, as I slip it quietly over the side of the boat.

"I saw that," says Mishomis.

"It's not that I don't trust you, Miisho, really I do. I just don't trust *her.*"

He laughs.

"I'm *not* superstitious," I say, looking about the boat to make sure that everyone is wearing a personal flotation device, and that each one is buckled. "It's just a reminder to myself to be cautious," I say, checking to make sure that the dog is not about to knock a relaxed five-year-old out of the boat. He is prone to dangling over the edge, singing, or to ride the bow when the waves are high, vying with the big dog for a face full of spray.

"I know that I have more control over my safety out here than she does," I announce, waving my arms through the opaque, cool, wet, dense air.

"You're right." The old man smiles.

Now the fog is so thick that we cannot see more than a few feet ahead. We hunker close to the rock bluffs of the shoreline, inching along slowly, barely above an idle. We are moving so slowly that the tiny motor occasionally sputters. I wonder how much water seeped into those fifty-five-gallon drums of gaso-line my grandfather has been using. He flips open the engine cover with one hand, while steering with the other, and puffs a bit of WD-40 into the carburetor. The rock cliffs and shoals faintly advance and retreat without regularity. The old man is steering us home by sheer memory. I reach into my other pocket for anything to help us survive out here if we don't make it back: seymuh, cough drops, matches, rosary beads. . . .

"There. See? There it is." He stops the motor, and we coast toward a black rock with a turtle painted on it, in reddish-ochre-colored exterior barn paint. "See? I put it there to find my way home when it's foggy. You just don't have any control over it, and sometimes you've got to find your way to the house, if the kids get cold or something. . . ."

I hug the child cuddled in my lap. I smell his head. I love the way my babies smell. Children don't say that they are hot or cold until it is too late, so we've got to pay attention to things like that and mandate temperature control measures for them, even if they complain. And he is complaining, that he doesn't need his jacket. But I know better, and I have worried for us out here.

The red turtle lies on its side, its head pointing to the left, out into the open water.

"This is where I turn to head straight to the island," he says. Then he yanks the pull cord on the engine and chuckles. Full speed ahead. He eases in to the dock, cutting the engine just in time. I step to the bow and pull the rope and clip from the dock railing.

From inside the small house, with food on the table, Ki-ishigokwe is the most beautiful woman I have ever seen. Her dance is endless and changing, for hours on end. I welcome the gift of her presence.

As I stare out the window, sandwich in hand, I reflect upon my years in college. I think about the experts and historians who have speculated about the meaning of the images my ancestors painted on the rocks. Some of them have stories. I've been told some of them. But my favorite piece of rock art on all of the shores of all of the lakes is the one that says, "Turn left."

He has a story about every crack in the rocks, every inlet, pebbly bay, and stretch of beach. He has camped each and every sheltered cove, alone or with family and friends. These are the miles of Lake Superior's least populated shoreline, since its fish supplies were decimated and the steamers disappeared, leaving empty villages. The impact upon families was immense. People lost their reason to be on the lake and stopped traveling north and south by water. People moved away and began marrying east to west, because that's how the roads went. The only roads around Lake Superior's easternmost limits were rugged labyrinths of logging trails. So the Indian language grew apart into north and south, and the art styles and all the other ac-

The Trout Lake

coutrements of community life grew apart into northern and southern counterparts. All this in just one-half of one small century . . . after centuries of lifetimes on this lake. Only a few stubborn souls remained.

"Right there, that's where James buried his dog. We made a marker."

"I want to see it."

"On the way back, if it's not too late."

"Did the dog die of old age?"

"Yes, right there with them."

"That's fortunate." What love, what care, to transport that adventurous old friend with them.

"Now where did that cross go? Some fellas climbed up and painted a cross on the rocks. It's probably faded by now."

We do not find the cross. Not this time. Nor do we return to the beloved dog's gravesite, with a doggie biscuit in a pocket, to feed its spirit . . . and ours.

We have pulled into one of my favorite coves, a tiny patch of sand at the back of a deep arm of the lake. The mouth of the stream that empties there is never the same on any given year.

"Why do they call it Indian Harbour?" I ask. He shrugs and points to a square in the ground made up of barely recognizable log humps.

"There used to be a log cabin here," he says, brushing at the leaves of a small maple growing in its center.

It was a silly question. Of course I know why it is called Indian Harbour. Who in their right mind wouldn't want to live in this incredible, hospitable place? It is a convoluted system of coves within coves and lakes within lakes, with vast areas of flat, usable land and gentle hills. It is a haven within a cliff-bound and mountainous shoreline. Its underwater cliffs and its islets have always been perfect structure and spawning grounds for fish. Animals thrive in its gentleness. People thrived here, too.

I feel a little bit empty not completely understanding the history of this place. Even Mishomis and his cohorts came too late to understand it fully. There was a break in continuity.

"The stream looks pretty dry," I say. "Let's walk up to the meadow?"

"Which meadow is that?" he asks.

"Oh, maybe I'm mixed up. I thought this was it. Because in that other cove over there, the lake acts very strange. . . ." I had been certain of my bearings only moments ago, but I deferred to the old man's experience and judgment.

"The trail is on the other side. Little Guy can't cross the stream walking on that log. It's OK for you or me, but it's too far for him to balance."

"Let's move the boat then," says Mishomis. So we climb back into the boat and row it ten feet up the beach.

"Make sure we stay on this side," says Mishomis, "because the fork comes in the other side there. It's almost like an island in the middle."

Now I am comfortable again, because I remember the fork, and I remember the places upstream where we can walk over each branch of water easily. Perhaps the old man has forgotten the vast meadow. After all, it's been years. We wind our way silently up the gentle slope for half an hour.

"Here's the meadow, Miisho. It has the tiniest stream running through it." It is one of my favorite places in the world, this big clearing full of moose tracks in the middle of the dense bush. I love to run through this meadow and swing my arms freely. It is always full of wildflowers.

"Well I'll be. . . . This is your meadow, eh?"

I am confused by his stature. I love this meadow. I can imagine *Anishnabe* women and children for generations back enjoying its openness.

"My brother and I used to bring a canoe up this stream here. . . ."

"No, not through this tiny stream."

"Yes! Through this stream here, up past the fork. We used to get out and drag it over the shallow spots. And then we used to paddle it through this lake here. . . ." He waves his hand over the meadow, a kilometer wide from top to bottom.

I've always known the meadow must flood at least once a year, otherwise it would fill with trees. But I cannot imagine it as a lake.

"It must have been a very shallow lake."

"Well, sure. It was a moose lake. But we could paddle the length of it . . . all the way to the next stream. We could paddle it up that stream, too, except when the water was low . . . all the way up to the next lake. It was a great trout lake."

I am dumbfounded. "OK. I believe you." Dumbfounded, not by the old man's memory or lack of it, but dumbfounded by the cyclical changes that happen in this watershed. I feel very small, and I feel that my presence on Lake Superior's shoreline is very brief. I cannot recall ever having seen water in this lake. And Grandfather has not been here for years. He cannot recall ever *not* seeing water in this lake. There is no constant here, and it will take three generations to tie together the events of this waterway.

The boy is too small to walk through the muckiest parts of the meadow to the next stream. We step from grass clump to grass clump, and he loses a shoe. We retrieve it and retreat to the driest end of the meadow. Mishomis, in the meantime, has gone to explore the next lake upstream, so that he can report on its existence. The child and I pick bunny tails, dried flower stalks from last year, their hard seeds sent windward last autumn. The remaining tufts are soft like cotton swabs, and we rub them around our eyes and mouths.

Yes, the lake is still there. The old man is shaking his head and chuckling in disbelief. "Some years we didn't have to get out and push at all."

"I believe you."

That night, as we pour over the maps, the boy stuffs a bunny tail into Misho's ear. There they are, all right . . . on the maps. Lakes.

"We had a lot of good meals of speckled trout out of that upper lake."

"I believe you."

The old man and the little boy have gone off around the cape, on some sort of adventure. I am free to work on my porcupine quill and sweetgrass baskets. This is my livelihood, and I am fortunate that my work is portable. I have made it clear to Grandfather that I cannot accompany him to the island unless I bring my work along. Unable to sit still and watch me, the two are jacketed up and off into the distance. They are too far away, too small to see, long before they round the cape. I know, because I keep running out to the end of the dock and peeking. I am jealous, because I know they will have fun. However, being alone is almost as much fun. I love having clear and continuous thoughts.

Manaboozhou's Basket

Making baskets is hard work. Two-thirds of the work involves gathering and processing the materials. I don't get many materials from this island. It comprises only about thirty acres, and its life forms are fragile and limited. It is a vast rock outcropping with mere pockets of soil on its convoluted surface. No porcupines live here, so I bring washed and sorted quills out to the island. While I gather a little bit of birch bark here, I have better sources elsewhere. The island is, however, my favorite place to gather spruce roots.

I use spruce roots to hold the baskets together. I use fine roots, especially for finish work, stitching sweetgrass in place. I also use fine roots to make designs on baskets in the shapes of flowers and animals, similar to porcupine quillwork. The largest roots I use are a little fatter than spaghetti. I use them to bind together the structural parts of large baskets.

I have learned, over the years, to make beautiful designs with the stitching. Putting something together with roots is difficult. First I make a small hole into the overlapped layers of bark, using an awl. I have a lot of different sizes and shapes of awls, which other Indian basket makers have given me over the years. Each one works in a different situation. They have become old friends to me, and I see the faces of the people who made them, every time I use them.

Before the bark layers have a chance to pull apart, I insert a sharpened piece of root into the hole and grab its tip on the other side with a pair of pliers. My favorite pliers are the ones that Mishomis makes for me out of green birch. They are supple and strong, but they do not scratch the bark. Sometimes, on a large basket, I have to brace and pull with my whole body.

These are the same roots and the same stitching techniques used to build birch bark canoes, but on a different scale. I've watched the men doing this work with heavy roots. But in the old days, it was women who did the finish stitching on canoes, because we were experienced and had the tools. Women knew exactly how to trim and shape the roots to get the least amount of resistance on a pull, how big to make the holes, so that the root would rip its host material just enough to make a snug fit. Basket makers knew when to work wet, when to work dry, when to stitch long, when to stitch short. . . . These things are all art forms. This expertise comes from a familiarity derived only from practice, from trial and error, from doing it wrong, then right, from experimentation and risk taking. . . .

It is said that Manaboozhou made the first basket. He made it out of desperation, as a birdcage. He was trying to transport some migratory birds from south to north, out of season. He had tried tucking warblers into the folds and pockets of his buckskin shirt. He pulled a fur-lined, hooded jacket over this, wrapped his arms around his tiny bundles, and bent forward into the oncoming northwest wind. After a few minutes of walking, the birds clawed and nipped at his wrists and hands. Wriggling free from the soft buckskin bundling, they emerged all at once from the underside of his overcoat. He swiped and pawed, but the birds were free, and they headed back south before he'd carried them into a dangerously cold climate.

No problem, thought Manaboozhou. Thrushes are among the first birds to return to the north. They are bigger and won't mind the cold so much. So Manaboozhou searched about and gathered several sweet-singing thrushes. He entwined the birds within some locks of his hair that had blown free in the harsh weather. Then he pulled the jacket hood over his head and bent into the north wind. After a few hours of walking, the birds clawed his forehead and pecked at his eyes.

"Ooow, ow!" he cried out. "You're pulling my hair!"

So, in frustration, the big, foolish man untangled the poor birds and sent them flying southward.

Now, word had spread among all species of birds and fowl that Manaboozhou was up to something unnatural. Birds began cooperating with one another for a few days. Predator and prey, for once, came freely within whispering distance of one another. The birds posted guards in the pine boughs and sent messengers ahead of Manaboozhou, as the spirit strode the southerly extremes of the continent, searching for birds. Yet all he encountered were seemingly empty forests. The birds were so well organized and so secretive.

Although Manaboozhou is a fool, he is an intelligent and creative fool. He knows a thing or two about birds.

So Manaboozhou set about fashioning a fine-meshed net of evergreen roots. He went to the shore of a lake, where the trees are shallow-rooted. Feeling his way out from the base of the tree, he carefully reached into the moist sand under a small root, following it down until it was as small and straight as he wanted it. Then he pulled. He lifted the root upward until its branched tips were as fine as thread. He repeated this procedure several times, taking care not to remove too many roots from any one tree. Then he clipped and sorted them by size.

Each root was then peeled right away, while fresh, each tiny skin being turned inside out. Finally, Manaboozhou fashioned a wide net. He camped out patiently, waiting for a dark, overcast day. The birds, he knew, did not see well in dim, flat light. Then Manaboozhou placed the net across a likely bird flyway.

This is how the spirit man outwitted the conspiring birds, for although his mission was absurd, it was driven by altruism. The birds were for a sick child.

Once several birds were trapped in the net, Manaboozhou balled up the whole thing and threw it over his shoulder. But almost immediately, the birds began to complain. They were thrown together, upside-down and right side-up, wings bent, feathers tousled, beaks poking into one another's ribs. The birds were very uncomfortable, and Manaboozhou, determined though he was to carry those poor birds into the frozen north, realized that he could not continue to make them suffer along the way. So he untangled the net and gently released the birds, one after another.

Despondent, he sat on a bluff halfway home, high above a swamp. He leaned back against a large birch tree and closed his eyes. That's when he heard it:

"Take me. Oooooooh. . . . take me."

He looked around, and then up. Must be the rustling of those few dried, brown leaves, still clinging to the tree, he thought. And he rested again, watching the small birds flit from tree to tree in the valley below.

"Take me. Oooooooh, use my gifts."

Manaboozhou closed his eyes again and listened hard.

"Take me. Oooooooh, use my bark."

There it was, all around him. Birch bark. He had ignored the obvious. One branch leaned down and tickled him with a wavering, papery piece of the bark. A warbler landed on a large, flat piece, lying on the ground. It had been dislodged by the wind only days ago.

So it was that Manaboozhou made the first basket out of birch bark and root bindings. Naturally, the trip northward with wildlife out of season was predictably disastrous. Still, it was by way of this disaster that Manaboozhou came to teach *Anishnabe* women and girls how to make baskets which is, of course, another story. And I hear the hum of the distant boat motor before it can pass completely through my mind on this particular day.

I have just finished the basket. It is an open berry- picking basket. Its long handle is embellished with quillwork. The sweetgrass trim along the basket and the handle is stitched in place with tiny spruce roots, each peeled and trimmed smooth. Every stitch is made with awl and pliers. There are no man-made materials in this basket. It could have been made by Manaboozhou himself.

I make this type of basket only rarely. The people who buy my baskets prefer needle-and-thread work, which is finer and prettier, though less sturdy. I defer to their perceptions of what a traditional Indian basket is. I make the old-style baskets for family and friends . . . and for my own peace of mind. I am the only person I know of who can still trim a basket this way, and I fret for the loss of the skill. It was acquired by Manaboozhou only as a result of great effort and foolishness. This lesson learned should not be wasted.

Superior has back bays and inlets that are so convoluted, so long and narrow, so bent back upon themselves, that one would hardly recognize them as part of the same huge lake. It is in these narrow backwaters that the lake shows characteristics that few people see. This is where the *michikiniibigag* migrate from the inland lakes and waterways to confer with Mishii Bizhou. The great swimming mountain lion is their friend and leader.

They are misfits, all of them. Monsters. So they live underwater, where they can disappear in a trace. The *michikiniibigag* are snakes, snakes of every size, shape, and color. They are benign snakes, mousers and bug-eaters for the most part. They are all good swimmers, especially the hog-nosed snakes. Hog-noses have been known to roll over and play dead on the surface of the water, mid-swim, when confronted by a canoe. It is an amazing and magical feat.

The Michikiniibigag

But the odd thing about these snakes is their antlers. Some have big, broad moose antlers. Others have tiny deer antlers. This causes them considerable trouble when they try to slither in and out of cracks in the earth, or under piles of leaves. Sometimes they get stuck. So they have altered their personalities to cope with their physical abnormalities. They behave less like snakes than most snakes. But they can't quite behave like large mammals. Big-footed caribou and clumsy moose have been known to step on their antlered brethren, when the *michikiniibigag* attempt to mingle. For these reasons, the poor monsters have been known occasionally to become cranky. Lately, they've only been coming out in the moonlight. They look an awful lot like an old twisted log with a few dead branches sticking up. But they're not. They are the *michikiniibigag.*

My Uncle Dick once told me about a *michikiniibig* that became so perturbed when it was sat upon by a moose that it vowed revenge. It combed the rivers, streams, and tributaries of the whole north shore of Lake Superior gathering support for its mission. They all came together at a designated back bay to confer with Mishii Bizhou. They hid together under a large shelf of algae bloom a little way out into the lake, where a meandering stream dumped valley silt over an underwater drop-off. They devised a plan.

Mishii Bizhou would cooperate by behaving himself and keeping the lake calm. He would flatter and distract the thunderbirds, so that they would make no ripples on the lake. Then he would call out like a great, lonesome moose: "Awoo-oo, awoo-oo . . . ooh, ooh, ooh!"

When the moose came rushing out for a shoreline drink and a little woo-pitching on this calmest of days, the *michikiniibigag* would push upward, all at once. The land would rise up below their buffoon feet and knock the ignorant, clumsy moose into the lake, noses first.

The plan worked pretty well. In fact, quite a few of the moose were flung head over heels into the lake, when the earth rose up, and those mountains around the lake were formed. That's why moose have resolved themselves to become such good swimmers. But some of the *michikiniibigag* were too small to heft their share of the landscape, so there are flats and valleys here and there.

The lake still sloshes from their effort. On calm days, in the longest and narrowest of bays, one can observe it rising and falling, about once every sixteen minutes. That is why, on short excursions, one should pull one's boat up well past the water line and tie it to a tree, even in the most protected bays. Those water monsters are pretty tricky.

The Michikiniibigag

M anaboozhou's patient wife, Minwaudeniimikwe, makes
batches of soap in early winter, when animal fat is most
available. She cooks up the butchering scraps out of doors in
a wide, deep clay pot, then strains out the solids and bits
with a long-handled willow and cattail sieve, made just
for that purpose. The fried bits will be sorted out later,
and the toughest bits given to her husband's two big
dogs. When the coals around the pot have cooled
down, and only the clay vessel retains its heat, she
adds to the barely liquid contents a thick and
pasty strained tea of hardwood ash. She mixes it
into the round-bottomed pot, smoothly, with a
slightly curved cedar paddle fashioned from
driftwood. When the two incompatible liquids
are bound together by the woman's sheer **Laundry Day**
physical force, she adds another strong bit of
tea of crow's mint to scent and temper the
soap. She readjusts the pot between the three
blackened stones that hold it up, searching for
a few remaining coals. Temperature is crucial.
Too hot won't work. Neither will too cold, so
she must work fast with the paddle to avoid
fetching coals from inside the house for finish-
ing the task.

Today there is a solid, wet snow on the
ground, deep enough and wet enough for mold-
ing the soap, so she doesn't have to make round
molds out of birch bark slipped from dead
branches. The cooled soap is packed into thick-
sided rectangular birch bark baskets, to protect it
from mice and other animals.

Each basket has a tight-fitting flat lid. Since the baskets were all made from supple, fresh bark, each is lovingly scraped with designs of waterfowl, animals, and
fish—all the *dodaimig,* or totems, protective animals that the
Anishnabeg use to identify their family lines. She adds a new

121

basket or two to the collection every few years or so, when the opportunity presents itself. *Anishnabe* women are notorious basket collectors, and Minwaudeniimikwe is as guilty as any of us. She loves not only her own handiwork, but that of her sisters as well. Each specializes in a slightly different style and form of decoration. Each basket maker recognizes the work of another at a mere glance.

Minwaudeniimikwe's soap baskets are kept on a storage-building shelf at chest level. She knows that any animals eager to eat soap for its fat content can climb the shelves if they want to, but she figures that there's no need to make it easy for them. So she never puts the soap on the bottom shelf, and she keeps it in a place that she enters frequently in order to keep creatures away from it. The perfume scent of the crow's mint helps keep animals away, too.

Today, Minwaudeniimikwe has been washing laundry in Lake Superior all morning. The suds have washed up on the beach in small fluffy bunches. All along the downwind shore, children have been dipping up handfuls and blowing them at one another. A few toddlers have rubbed suds in their hair, and parent's *tsk,* as the lake is too cold for the youngsters to plunge in for a rinse.

Minwaudeniimikwe is in the final stages of potty training her youngest child. So today, the bedding is flapping in the breeze. It is heavy and difficult to wash alone, especially in early summer's cold water. But she has sent her husband and children off on various missions. Manaboozhou's sole job today is to entertain a six-year-old. She has things to do, and free working time is a rare commodity.

After much heaving, draining, and twisting, she has managed to pull the heavy bedding over her head and flip it onto the clothesline. Her clothespins are store-bought, the kind with a metal spring, and although her husband complains profusely about the intrusive nature of such newfangled things, she really appreciates the modern invention. Whether he likes it or not, the metal and wood clips work as well as the kind

Manaboozhou makes for her out of green wood, and she doesn't have to pester him to make new ones. Living in modern times has its advantages.

Now Minwaudeniimikwe washes Manaboozhou's favorite wool sweater, his lucky fishing sweater. It is worn thin from so much wear and washing. Another modern invention. She notices that he is selective about what is acceptable about life in the present, and what is not. The sweater will have to be replaced eventually, and she will have to coax her husband into some new type of fabric. Such are the tender and loving trials that Manaboozhou and his wife put one another through as the centuries move on.

They are back from their adventures, my two boys, the big one and the little one. Even before they reach the dock, they are standing up in the boat and shouting, "Look what we brought you!"

The boat is full of flowers. I feel like a South Pacific islander, in spite of the red hooded sweatshirt I have pulled on, and even though my feet and legs are cold. This morning I boiled potatoes for salad, and then I scrubbed the starch off of the pot with fine beach sand. The lake has left my extremities numb. Still, I've gotten so much done while they've been gone, that now I am eager for their boisterous company. And this is such a visual treat. . . .

Flowers and Kisses

Grandfather stands protruding from the heaping flowers like a princess, arms upraised and outspread, as the boat glides up to the dock. He panics, turns, and bends down to lift the motor just in time, as he crosses the drop-off into the shallows. I run up to lean out and away from the dock, to grab the rope at the front end of the boat. Just as I stretch out over the water, my big St. Bernard cross leaps from the bow, throwing the boat off sideways. I run back down the length of the dock, to where I can leap off into the sand. Then I wade into the lake to retrieve my floating mass of flowers. We are all excited by the giving and receiving of surprise, like children on Christmas morning.

The dog barks and leaps after me, as I wade out, waist deep, beside the tied-up boat. My hooded sweatshirt is heavily soaking up water, as I bury my face in the flowers, breathing up the fragrance. The front of the boat is filled with apple blossoms. The rear is filled with purple lilacs. Both are in full bloom.

They have been off and away, exploring the decrepit, nearly invisible remains of the old fishermen's cabins, looking for useful treasures . . . old stove bolts without too much rust, an old metal net float to be converted into a soap dish, an old elixir bottle that still smells of turpentine (probably part of its original contents) . . . wonderful things to an old man and a boy. The remote fishing villages and even more remote outposts lasted well into the first half of the twentieth century. It was a different lake then, and the two of them have been reliving it.

"Where did you get *those?*" I ask.

"Bedbug Harbour."

"You went that *far?*" I am amazed. I look around. It is dead calm, and it was a perfectly safe trip. Yet where did the day go? No wonder I finished the potato salad before they returned!

Now the old-fashioned lilacs, my favorite, and the ancient, rare apple varieties' blooms are coming up from the boat to the dock, into my arms, bundle after bundle. They have been handled so carefully and so lovingly that no branches are broken. Tall, white plastic buckets are filled with the flowering branches. We take turns posing between the buckets on the porch, while one stands in the doorway snapping pictures. Lilacs on the left, apple blossoms on the right, Lake Superior, two dozen loons, and a few small islands in the background. Smile! Snap.

The buckets are lined up around the tiny, one-room house. I walk down the shoreline to get a look, then insist upon being taken out in the boat to get the full effect.

So this is early summer in Bedbug Harbour. Not even the bedbugs are left to enjoy it. The natural harbor was a haven for various intermarried Swedish and Ojibwe fishermen before the fish were mostly gone. It was named for the pests who drove away its stubbornnest of seasonal residents. The trees must have been a joy for water-bound wives decades before. Bringing saplings to such remote spots was practically an act of heroism. And every ancient and wild apple I have seen on the shores of the big heat-holding lake bears fruit consistently. What joy! And this joy still belongs to me and my family . . . I am knee deep in it.

Mishomis and Little Guy are kissing me on each cheek, and we are all still laughing. They are such lovers, these two. Mishomis, I know, has always been a ladies' man, and it is hard for me to imagine him alone in his old age. I remember how he used to kiss my Grandmother, long and hard, in the kitchen . . . her back arched against the handle of the indoor water pump, pushing it downward. The pump would gurgle, as the vacuum pushed up in the pipe. The old folks had a pretty good vacuum going, too.

My mother and father used to kiss that same way, long and hard, every day in the kitchen. I figured they did it so well because they had such good role models. I hope that my own children will carry on the family tradition. . . .

Actually, according to Ojibwe oral tradition, love and passion are a significant part of our heritage. Manaboozhou, it is said, was quite a ladies' man. Of course, it is Minwaudeniimikwe whom he eventually wooed, and by whom he was also wooed, with the intent of staying together for eternity. We joke that she is the only one tolerant enough to put up with him but, in reality, they are together for *passion* as well as practicality. Manaboozhou's wife's house is always filled with flowers, especially after he does something a little more foolish than usual. We know that he has incurred bee stings more than once, sticking his face into armloads of flowers. And his wife always makes him apologize to the bees for not being more careful. He is both child and man, at the same time, and this she loves about him.

I love this about my grandfather, too.

Flowers and Kisses

Once, I was being given a tour of a Michigan maritime museum by its director. When we came to the birch bark canoe display, I launched into quite a lecture. I explained what was used to bind things in place. I demonstrated how one had to constantly lick one's thumb and fingers when smoothing the sticky pitch into place. I explained that the pitch was tempered with tallow, to make it meltable and flowable, which is why birch bark canoes were always parked in the shade or stored underwater. I showed how the functional elements of the design were translated into a pretty pattern. After all, nobody wanted to go out in the water in something unless it *looked* like it was well made and would float. Confidence is a big part of one's relationship with a small watercraft.

Flying Pigs

Outside the museum was a fair-sized cedar log on sawhorses. Part of its interior had been cut away to a width of about a foot.

"What's that?" I asked.

"It's a dugout canoe."

I looked at my butt. I looked back at the canoe. No way. . . .

"Tight fit." I commented.

"A volunteer has been making it for us. He just wants to show the kids how hard it is to make one of these."

She had a point. But they'd been robbed. All of them. They'd been robbed. Robbed of the opportunity to grow up with old growth and virgin timber. They didn't know, any of them, that cedars get hollow when they get really big. The outside stays solid and strong. Making a dugout canoe was hard work, all right, but not as hard as whittling a solid green log.

Such problems occur when there is loss in continuity. People are robbed, robbed of their heritage, robbed of the common sense that comes with knowledge passed on. Keepers of history are sometimes forced to learn from trial and error, rather than from the mistakes and successes of their elders.

Too many years ago, when I was still a child, a huge, hollow cedar tree fell down from the edge of our island into Lake Superior. It lay wedged firmly and immovable between rock outcroppings, just past the *waukegon*. It stayed wet and was struck by waves intermittently when the wind was up. Mishomis, my uncles, and my father all decided that it would be best to let Superior properly take the bark from its outside and wear it smooth in all the right places, before the men would put the tree to its designated use. So, for several years, we children wandered past the old log cabin to check on the progress of the fallen cedar that would some day become our dugout canoe.

One cool, calm morning, all of the men decided that they had procrastinated nearly to the point of loss of the resource to the elements. It wasn't such a bad day for hard physical labor, and it was time to finally take action. So, after pouring fresh water into the coffee pot, percolating its soggy grounds a second time, and downing the results of their efforts, they were just about ready to take on their manly mission. Out of sight in the boathouse, their general rummaging for tools was surpassed only by their cursing of one another for their overall slovenliness and lack of organization, as well as disparagement of one another's judgment in terms of which tools to pile on top of one another and hang in front of one another as the years had passed. . . .

Now, through infinite thumping and a general knowledge of old cedar trees from their collective logging experiences, the men ascertained that the tree's hollow center was long enough to make a full-sized canoe. They also decided at what point each extremity of the trunk became solid again, to form the ends of the vessel. So they set about sawing, all of them like termites on a stump.

Now their calculations had been surprisingly correct, except for the error in judgment that caused Uncle Bill to saw off the base of the tree too high up, resulting in a hollow with no point at one end of the canoe. Mishomis insisted that he knew how to manufacture an end to the canoe, using fresh cedar strips and pitch, just like certain parts in a birch bark canoe. So the men deferred to the judgment of their father-in-law and father and continued on with the project. We children milled at a safe distance. They had laughed at the first error, but grownups could get downright cranky if miscalculations piled up.

Once the log was freed of its ends and trimmed of branches, it was rolled into the lake. With their boots pulled off and their socks tossed in wads, the men rolled up their pant legs and coaxed the log down the shore, nearer to the boathouse full of tools, and the kitchen full of women. It was waterlogged, but still floated.

The men decided to halve the trunk the long way while it was still wet, hoping that the swelling would work to their advantage. It did not, but they were in a particular mindset, and who knows when they would all be there together again, so they proceeded. They drove hard, triangular-shaped wooden wedges into the log, along both sides, until the beast split. Then they pried and heaved with every tool they had, until the four of them had the bulk of the log pulled apart. Grandfather set about hacking through the few connecting strips of wet cedar that stubbornly remained in place, and the men fell away under the weight of their respective halves when the last one was cut. The fellows decided that they had the ingredients for two dugouts, but voted to concentrate on only one, rather than push their luck.

The work that followed was hard . . . and fun. The soft punk wood was scooped out of the hollow center of the half log. Then they built a hot beach fire. The men and children had been gathering hard, dry beaver logs along the beach, each about the girth of a baseball bat. These were stuck, tip only, into the fire, a few at a time, to create burning tools. Eventually, the inside of the log was burned and scraped smooth and clean. The final product was thin, light, and strong . . . except one end was missing.

To fashion a makeshift laminated end for the dugout, Mishomis cut a fair-sized live cedar from way up the hill behind the house. He had recruited my sister to help carry it down, and then he taught her how to peel it. I could tell that she really didn't want to do it, but she did as she was told. Oh, how we loved to watch my oldest sister work! It was a form of benign revenge few people know. . . . "Get me the turpentiiine . . ." she'd hissed in my direction, when the job was done. And as the pecking order goes, I did as I was told, finding an old rag for her to clean her hands, too.

Mishomis took a small, heavy axe and began splitting long fans of cedar splints from the green log. Pulling, shaping, and smoothing them was a job he trusted to no one else. I remember, he still had mostly dark hair then, cut short. All of the men had crew cuts then. I remember the smooth, pretty shape of their heads as they bent over their work. Mishomis had work-related scars on his head, and a story to go with each of them.

The "boys," as Mishomis called the men, had crushed and melted the ingredients for pitch glue. There had been considerable discussion about which type of ash made the longest-lasting glue, but after an honest look at the probable seaworthiness of their craft, they decided that it didn't much matter. . . .

Still, the finished product was quite impressive. It was several days before the laminate makeshift bow of the canoe was placed onto the body of the beast. The laminate had to cure, and the half log still had to dry. For us children, the final assembly was anticlimactic. We'd lost interest, as the men obsessed over smoothing and sanding the surfaces of the canoe. Finally, it was painted a god-awful green with a mixture of old enamel leftovers from the boathouse.

After testing the wide, wobbly, uneasy craft, the grownups decided that it was the kids' canoe. And, they put safety restrictions on it: no farther than three meters from shore, no more than two people, and we had to wear life preservers at all times. Bummer. Just to make sure we didn't get stranded in the thing, Mishomis screwed a large metal eyelet for towing into its one solid end. After a season of wobbly adventures, we children christened the dugout the Water Pig and scrawled its name on one side in permanent magic marker.

While the Water Pig did not paddle well, it certainly towed well. This particular trait came to dominate the craft's personality, and we found ourselves begging the adults to tow us around the islands and reefs in "The Pig." Since the landscape around Misho's house is treacherous to fast-moving vehicles, the family's outboard motors tended to top out somewhere between nine and a half and fifteen horsepower. I don't think my father and uncles ever had the nerve to ease into full throttle when the Water Pig was in tow. But we felt like we were flying.

Some years later, my father brought one of his flatbed farm trucks loaded with lumber and hardware to the end of the road. The end of the road, of course, was not the edge of the lake. So we teenagers carried load after load of lumber to the rocky shore. Then we carried the boat and our supplies to the shore. Dad took an advance team of lumber unloaders with him to the island, leaving the rest of us to swat mosquitoes on the mainland, between bouts of loading up the boat. It felt like it took all day. Our hearts sank every time he rounded the cape without us.

We called him the Anal Retentive Carpenter, my father. He did everything painstakingly well. He wanted each and every creation to last. Rebuilding was not in his vocabulary. He had various projects in mind for this lumber, which he had cut, milled, and barn-dried himself. The most immediate of his goals was to replace Mishomis's sagging outdoor picnic table.

My dad rarely used nails. He had a propensity for bolting things together, in case they had to be taken apart, or moved, or modified for another use. Work was always in his vocabulary.

The top of the picnic table was removable, and before anybody even had a chance to serve a meal on it, my brother convinced Dad to take it off and bolt a homemade rudder onto its underside, using countersunk screws, so as to keep the table surface flat. A notch was cut into one end of the bracing underneath, and a large metal eyelet for towing was screwed into place. From the top of the picnic table lid, holes were bored to screw in a perfectly centered pair of size twelve and a half Converse All Star high-top sneakers. Black ones. In a stroke of genius I hate to give him credit for, my brother one day crawled under the picnic table with his pocket knife, where he lay on his back and crudely carved into the wood: WATER PIG II.

And so the adventures continued. Now even the dogs could fly, as long as we sat down and held them and cooed to them. Unfortunately, out of ten kids, two of us turned out to have feet that were not size twelve and a half. We littlefoots rode the picnic table lid standing upright in the high-tops anyway, filling the void with wadded up socks. This worked well, until one time when the boat motor stalled. I tried to pull in the slack and then let it back out gradually once the motor started up again. But somehow my hand got tangled in the rope, and I lurched forward when there was no slack left to ease out. The towrope yanked me right out of those Converse All Stars, and I landed face first on the lid of the picnic table. Among my siblings who witnessed the event there are those who claim that I actually did a front flip before landing. While this particular detail has become institutionalized within our family history, it is, in fact, pure fabrication. I know, because I was there. And they are a disreputable bunch of storytellers, each and every one of them.

Anyhow, that's how my nose was broken. I wouldn't mind so much, except that, thirty-some-odd years later, I still receive Christmas cards addressed to Water Pig III.

As I said, my dad always bolted things in place, in case he wanted to remove a part of something later . . . or parts . . . or tennis shoes specifically. I guess he'd lost his confidence in that particular small watercraft.

Space is at a premium in a one-room cabin, so we tend to condense and consolidate. Mishomis, however, tends to scatter and replicate. So, over the years, I watched my grandmother, and then my mother and aunties, mix things together into one container to save space. That is how our family invented shampoo soup. We mix the odds and ends of various shampoo brands together into one unbreakable container. Shampoo soup has, over the decades, remained a rather consistent fragrant minty green, although the opacity of the mixture has varied. It is, in fact, the nicest shampoo any of us has ever used, and if we could replicate it, we'd market it.

This small island and its tiny buildings have been, at various times in my life, overflowing with family and friends, especially children. In spite of Lake Superior's awesome scale, the island is a safe place for children. There just isn't any place else for them to go, and there are no electrical appliances, cars, or strangers to protect them from. We teach our children the basics of swimming and water safety before they can walk, and we have a wealth of traditional stories that are preventive in nature. Lord knows, the grownups scared the pants off of *me* on a regular basis. On the other hand, we grow to love, rather than fear, things that other people avoid, like cold, deep water or pitch black nights . . . or outhouses in the moonlight, whose paths are traversed by ghosts, cannibals, and hungry bears. . . .

Shampoo Soup

At night and on cold or rainy days, we pack bodies into every building. The kitchen camp has a big double bed, and we pull foldaways and mattresses out of the rafters of the boathouse. In the rafters of the kitchen camp, several extra, never-used cedar doors are laid in place side to side, creating a platform. One can stand on a chair to pull down a handmade rope ladder, and a few nervous boys can spend a motionless night pressed together in sleeping bags. There is a stack of yellowed comic books up there, and a forbidden magazine or two.

The log cabin sleep camp is full of big double beds, and we have no qualms about stuffing four to a bed. During the nighttime, foldouts fill the walkways, and one must crawl from bed to bed to go out to pee. The single oil lamp's chimney is usually blackened from children's attempts to turn up the flame for card games. The fireplace is rarely used, as the place stays warm from body heat.

Some years the toad population explodes, and on certain warm summer nights, the path from the kitchen to the sleep camp is full of toads. Children are given a torch and are cautioned not to step on the little things. To this day, when a grownup announces, "Time for bed!" a small child will respond, "Don't step on the toads!"

The weakest children in the pecking order are expected to use sleeping bags on the cedar platforms in the bathhouse. This is actually a pretty nice spot, because the hot water tank from the sauna keeps it cozy. It can't hold more than two children, and there are no big kids to accuse little ones of snoring. And you get your own flashlight, which is practically a god-like status in my family. The bathhouse smells pretty good from the soap, too.

The bathhouse is a treat when the weather is cold, but bathing in the lake is the easiest, the most fun, and the greatest test of stamina. It is an event that involves a lot of dares, along with a few leaps or intentional shoves off the end of the dock.

My parents and their siblings were excellent crowd control specialists in their day. We knew that they contrived rules and regulations behind our backs, and we referred to them as the Generals. So on warm, sunny days, rather than fight with us individually, they declared a universal bath time, and we all washed up at once, in front of the kitchen camp. Boys on one side of the dock, girls on the other. Nobody really cared if anybody peeked, except the five-through-ten-year-olds, who became temporarily obsessed with privacy. In fact, once, when a large, fat frog was discovered on the female side of the dock during wash-up time, I scrambled up and across the planks, dove at my brother, and shoved it down the front of his bathing suit. He chased me down the stony beach until he was able to shove the poor thing into the back of my drawers. . . .

We always used Ivory, the soap that floats, and anyone caught dropping it in the beach sand had penance to pay, because the whole bar of soap would get like sandpaper. So, if we blindly tossed a bar of soap across the dock to a crowd of the opposite sex, we always chose to err toward deep water. Often, somebody had to swim out for it, because Lake Superior *never* sends a lost item back to shore in a timely manner. And, if Lake Superior had gifted us with sun-warmed top water, and it was nice enough to shampoo, there was a whole new meaning to "pass the soup."

"Underhand or overhand?"

"Just put the lid on it first, and try not to hit me in the head."

My sister washes her short hair every day that she is here, rain or shine. She makes a quick head dunk in the cold lake, then lathers up. Then she stands at the very end of the dock, and one of her kids, who is taller than she is, pours a pot of warm water over her head. It is a quick and easy procedure, except for the part where they feign Samurai sword chops across the back of her neck while her eyes are closed. I've never told her about this, as, being a younger sibling, I still enjoy it when someone else challenges her authority and violates her dignity. When we were younger, she had the longest hair in the family, and she flaunted it.

Quiet Time

My hair is still long, so it takes a long time to dry. I don't wash it unless it's warm enough outside to dry it in the sunshine, or cold enough to fire up the woodstove. Today, I have heated up two roasting pans full of lake water on the propane burners and set them out on the picnic table, where I can spill and slosh. As I wrap my head in a big towel, I am grateful that no big kids are around to run up and mercilessly twist the towel as tightly as they can, under the auspices of helping me squeeze the water out. And, I am certain, they feign Samurai sword chops across the back of my neck when my eyes are closed.

Mishomis and Little Guy have been curled up indoors, on the big bed. The old man was reading a book of short stories. Grandfather has dozed off, and the five-year-old is propped up against his ribcage, intrigued by a comic book. We've read each one to him over and over, so he knows the stories and dialogue that go along with the pictures.

I drag a small mattress out into the sunshine on the dock. I've worked hard, and I deserve quiet time while my hair dries. I come inside to liberate the book from the sleeping man's hand. He had found it while rummaging around under an immense pile of pillows on the top shelf of a closet. "Well, I haven't seen this old friend in over thirty years," he had chuckled. And I was too embarrassed to admit that it was I who had stuffed the old hardbound volume under there for safekeeping some thirty-five years before, forgetting about it ever since.

I lie down in the sun and go right for the middle of the book, where I know I will find my favorite story, "Ball-o-Fat," by Guy De Maupassant. I figure that reading it will be a lot more fun, now that I'm all grown up.

Just as I begin to read, I catch movement out of the corner of my eye. There, in front of the sleep camp, is a large female caribou. She seems to be watching me intently. I assume she is about to swim across to the next island, but she nibbles a bit of grass and walks down the beach toward me. My arm is falling asleep, so I shift a little, and she moves into the trees by the path between buildings. She heads along the path, comes out next to the kitchen window, watches me for a while, then continues on the path toward the outhouse. There, she disappears into the trees.

I read for a while, and then I notice her out of the corner of my other eye, on the point at the water's edge, staring back at me. Once again, she glides back into the trees.

A few minutes later, she appears to my right again, by the sleep camp. Then she disappears and eventually emerges to the left, at the point.

This continues for half an hour. I wonder what she wants. She's been hanging around for days, surprising us on the outhouse path, peeking in the windows during dinner. So I move inside, worried that I am interfering with her business at hand.

I give up on Guy De Maupassant and decide to do some indoor chores, so I can keep an eye out the windows for my curious friend. She returns and munches grass a few feet from the kitchen window. I know that she likes this spot because it is out of the wind. One year, she had a calf against this side of the house. Mishomis had found it both delightful and vexing, because, although he was flattered by her comfort level there, he chose to give up listening to the radio for a few days, out of fear that he'd disturb her.

"Miisho, wake up!" I whisper. We watch the caribou as it grazes back down the path and into the trees. My little boy begins to drag a chair across the room to a window, squawking loudly for a better view.

"Shhhhh . . ." we insist. "Don't scare it away." But this is the wrong thing to say to a five-year-old who is in need of a nap, and the boy responds by screaming defiantly. The more we shush, the more he yells.

This ruckus has attracted the caribou's attention and, to our delight, she comes back to see what kind of animal is making all that noise. This is fine, until she clambers up onto the porch and sticks her head into the open door that faces the lake. As she sniffs at our household smells, we giggle. Then we realize that her antlers are stuck in the doorway. She has satisfied her curiosity and steps back. Clack! She tilts her head and tries again. Clack!

I am not too worried at first, because I figure caribou are used to getting their antlers out of tight places. They move silently through the woods back and forth behind our house and outbuildings. We rarely even hear the snap of a twig. However, I soon realize that her next strategy is to walk forward, into the room. She does this slowly, observing the details of our lives. Each time she turns her head one way or another inside the narrow one-room building, I am grateful that her antlers do not strike the dish cupboards or the warming bins above the woodstove. One branch of antler brushes against a dishtowel hanging above the sink, but the soft cloth stays in place on the wire. I am suddenly painfully aware of the clutter we have stationed above our heads as a matter of routine. I am terrified that a sudden noise will panic the animal and cause it to lunge inside the small room.

We are frozen in fear, on our knees, on top of the mattress, backs against the wall. I can feel Mishomis's marine radio against the back of my head. I pray that it is off and will not crackle. I am afraid that my son will wiggle or scream, but I realize that he has sensed the severity of the situation and is frozen in place with the adults. Still, I am afraid to release the tight clamp of my hand against his open mouth. I feel his breath, hot and short, on the top finger of my hand. I am afraid to turn my head, but I think I see light reflecting off of Mishomis's glasses. He's not doing anything brave, and I am grateful.

The caribou is larger than a deer, but smaller than a moose. Still, she fills up the kitchen, and I am stunned at how far her strong, steamy breath travels across the room. I am afraid to blink against it, as it strikes my face. She walks steadily toward us. I memorize every detail, the long white hairs of her neck ruff, the speckling of her snout, the dog-like crust in the corners of her eyes. . . . Oh, where is the dog?

I see our frozen reflections in one of her large eyeballs, as she slowly turns and heads toward the open door on the other side of the house. *Please,* don't get stuck, I think, as she ambles to the door. Her huge hooves sound like cowbells on the wooden floor. Two tries. It takes her two tries to walk out the door, dipping her head and tilting her antlers a bit, backing up blindly and doing it again.

Even after her immense buttocks and those huge hind feet are safely out the door, we stay frozen. I begin to relax my muscles a little, when she stops and urinates on the concrete pad outside the door. I realize it could have been worse. We stand in the doorway, where a few drops of caribou urine have spattered into the dust of the doormat, and we watch. She nuzzles a half-eaten apple on the picnic table. No interest. She nibbles at a washcloth on the clothesline, leaving its corner wet.

She walks over to the boathouse and sticks her head in the open door. "Oh, no, not again!" Mishomis laughs. The head tilts and glides out smoothly. Next, she stops at the outhouse and pokes in her snout. When she withdraws it, several layers of toilet paper freshly bitten from the roll are protruding from her mouth. She chews and swallows. Then she heads up the path and disappears like an apparition into the spruce and balsams behind the outhouse.

As I sit on the edge of the bed, I am shaking from being frozen for so long and from the adrenaline in my system. I notice that I still have a clamp on the back of Little Guy's T-shirt.

"Wonder Dog!" I call out softly, and she emerges sleepily from under the bed. Then, fully awake, she sniffs at every footfall on the kitchen floor.

"So," Mishomis smiles, "did you do anything interesting today?"

"Uh, I tried to read Guy De Maupassant."

Little Guy is jumping up and down on the bed. "Don't call me *Guee!* I hate when you say my name that way." Of course. Business as usual. What are we gonna do next?

"I think I'll go rinse the doormat, before it dries."

The feats that we attribute to our bumbling teacher, Manaboozhou, are many and varied. Powerful as the son of a
spirit, yet flawed in judgment due to his mother's human
heritage, he is the subject of many stories and the butt of
many jokes. Still, he deserves our respect.

Today, Grandfather has taken us up the coast to
where the great man Manaboozhou lies in repose,
close to shore. Here he rests between escapades on
the great lake. Mishomis motors along the cliffs, to
the northernmost side of the rock outcropping,
where we can see Manaboozhou clearly outlined
against the horizon of the lake. His head is
thrown back, as he pants for breath upon completion of some amazing feat. The wake from
our small motor ripples around his knuckles,
and his big feet flop out to both sides.

When Stones Walk the Earth

Manaboozhou is surrounded by deadly reefs,
barely visible until one is almost upon them.
Sometimes, out of nowhere, great swirls of wind
rise up and blow the curious off course. It is
Lake Superior's job to protect him when he rests
here. His beloved Grandmother who raised him
is long gone, and there is no one around powerful enough to look after Manaboozhou. So we for-
give the lake and the winds their treachery. The
West Wind, after all, is his father.

Few people dare visit Manaboozhou when he
sleeps. But we are family, and Epanigishimoog has
given us his blessings. Mishomis guides the tiny
boat to a familiar spot in the rocks. We disembark
and tie up to an outcropping.

We climb up the back of his immense head and perch
on his wide forehead. I brush at the grass and small
cedars that are growing in his hair. "Oh, Manaboozhou,
you've been sleeping so long that your hair is a mess." Manaboozhou, after all, is known to be a bit vain about his hair.

We stare out over the long expanse of the lake. This is the longest unbroken stretch of open water on the lake, with no islands or peninsulas to break the wind. This is where Manaboozhou jumped across the lake the long way, just to prove to his brothers that he could do it. We begin to tell the boy stories of Manaboozhou's adventures, mistakes, and accomplishments, the things he does when he is not resting here, stone still.

"How come *I* never see him when he moves?" the small boy asks.

"You will. Just be patient."

"Do *you* ever see him when he's not stone?"

"Oh, yes. Lots of times. He can change himself into lots of different animals and different things. You have to learn how to recognize him."

"*When* will I learn to recognize him?"

"You'll learn it a little at a time, as you get older."

"I *never* get to see him move. Why did he turn into stone for so long that he's got trees on his head?"

I look down at my own hands and fidget. This is a tough subject.

"Some people say that he turned to stone and stayed that way because he is unhappy about the things that have happened to the *Anishnabe* people."

"Who are the *'Nishnabe* people?"

"Us. People like us."

"What happened bad to us?"

"Nothing. Don't worry. We won't let anything bad happen to you."

"Will he ever stop being stone again? Will he ever stop not moving?"

"He moves, I told you. He'll never stop moving and doing things. He'll always be here for us."

Mishomis changes the subject and starts telling us, in detail, about the time he rode a caribou across the lake. He describes holding on to the animal's long white neck ruff, and then pushing himself back and away when he felt the caribou's front hooves hit solid ground underwater. He pulls down his glasses and shows us the scar on his forehead, where a back hoof grazed him.

The water was calm then, like today, and his brother had pulled up alongside the swimming animal in a motorboat, while Mishomis leaped spread-eagle onto its back. It is easy to visualize this event, because a caribou swims so high out of the water, and Mishomis is prone to sudden, unexpected, and wild moves. (He is the subject of many stories and the butt of many jokes. Still, he deserves our respect.)

I don't think any of us have ever had the nerve to tell Mishomis that, although riding the poor caribou is an amazing feat, we think it was an incredibly stupid and cruel thing to do. Yet it must show on my face, because he says, apologetically, "I was younger then." He waves his arm up and down the coast, then across the lake. "This was all ours. We never thought the freedom would end. We did things we would never do today." I nod my understanding. The five-year-old sitting between us has already shown signs of being fearless and wildly experimental.

I look down at his face and realize the boy does not understand that Miisho merely rode the caribou across a narrow channel from one island to another. He thinks that the old man miraculously rode the animal across the length of the lake, as far as the eye can see.

Long after Mishomis is gone, and after I am gone, as a man he will tell the story of his great grandfather who rode across Lake Superior on the back of a swimming caribou. Those people will not know Mishomis, and they will begin to confuse those distant boyhood memories of his with the fantastic exploits of Manaboozhou himself. So the stories will continue. . . .

I kiss the top of my boy's head. I bury my nose in his crew cut and inhale his soft smell deeply. "He'll move again soon, I promise."

When Stones Walk the Earth